# DEATH OF THE COUCH POTATO'S WIFE

*Christy Barritt*

DEATH OF THE COUCH POTATO'S WIFE
BY CHRISTY BARRITT
Published by Lighthouse Publishing of the Carolinas
2333 Barton Oaks Dr., Raleigh, NC, 27614

ISBN 978-0-9847655-9-1
Copyright © 2012 by Christy Barritt
Cover design by Bluetail Books & Design:
www.bluetailbooks.com
Book design by Anna O'Brien www.behindthegift.com

Available in print from your local bookstore, online, or from the publisher at: www.lighthousepublishingofthecarolinas.com

For more information on this book and the author visit:
www.christybarritt.com

All rights reserved. Non-commercial interests may reproduce portions of this book without the express written permission of Lighthouse Publishing of the Carolinas, provided the text does not exceed 500 words. When reproducing text from this book, include the following credit line: "*Death of the Couch Potato's Wife* by Christy Barritt published by Lighthouse Publishing of the Carolinas. Used by permission."

Library of Congress Cataloging-in-Publication Data
Barritt, Christy.
*Death of the Couch Potato's Wife* / Christy Barritt 1st ed.

Printed in the United States of America

# Dedication

This book is dedicated to anyone who's ever lived in suburbia and experienced the joy of a homeowners' association and nosy neighbors.

A special thank you goes out to: Pat Mathias, Kellie Yates Miller, Stephanie Ludwig, Pamela Trawick, Laura McClellan, Kate Hinck, and Sharon Lavy. Your input was invaluable!

# 1

"This is called breaking and entering."

Babe, my neighbor, waved her hand in the air in a laid-back way that made me wonder if she'd been a cat burglar in her pre-senior citizen discount days. "We're not breaking anything."

My neck muscles clenched tighter. "How about the law?"

"Nonsense, Laura. We're just being neighborly." Babe used that word a lot, including when gossiping and borrowing lawn equipment from other people's sheds—without their permission. My husband and I had been the recipients of her neighborly deeds on many occasions.

Babe and I stood on the porch of Candace Flynn's house, staring at her front door. Though it was only 3 p.m., the crisp winter sun was already beginning its descent, and a glare of light caught on the glass atop the door, nearly blinding us. All the other neighbors on the cul-de-sac seemed to be occupied at the moment because no one else stirred. Most of them were working or at afternoon tot time at the local gym.

Sure, Candace's husband had been out of town all week on a golf outing. But was that really an excuse for the mostly dry, yellowing grass in her front yard to be uncut with wisps of some kind of winter weed waving to everyone who passed? Or for the garbage cans to remain curbside for two days? For various flyers, once stuffed behind her door handle, to now litter the stoop?

Even more disturbing than the aesthetic no-nos of her yard was the fact that the storm door, which had been closed just yesterday, now flapped open.

And there was the small fact that no one had seen the woman in two days—and Candace always made herself known. She wasn't even answering her cell phone, which usually appeared to be glued to her ear.

All of these things left me with three thoughts. First, I considered that maybe Candace had spontaneously taken off on a trip herself. I couldn't fault her for doing so, because I knew her husband never cut her any slack. If she was going to go, it should be now, while he was out of town. My second thought was that perhaps she'd decided to abandon all responsibilities for the week. I couldn't blame her for that either, though, if that were the case, I at least wanted to help Candace by sending my husband Kent over to cut the wispy grass. The third possibility, and this was the one I didn't want to consider: What if she'd run into trouble? A heart attack with no one around to help? A home invasion that had left her tied up inside with the front door flailing open?

Perhaps the correct way to be neighborly was by calling the police.

But Babe insisted I'd lived in Chicago too long. She said this was the way things were done here in small-town America. She said that neighbors checked on each other.

I was no expert on the subject and Babe, by all accounts, was. At seventy years old, she knew nearly three times more about life than I did. And when I moved here nine months ago, I knew nothing—nothing—about small towns. All I knew was that this small town was actually named Boring. To top it off, the sign at the end of the road labeled our neighborhood Dullington Estates.

When my husband first told me, I thought he was joking.

Nope. Boring, Indiana, was as real as they came.

I nodded toward Candace's door and glanced back at Babe, who was all decked out in a jean jacket, a Rolling Stones T-shirt and Converse tennis shoes. The woman had moxie, I'd give her that. We'd already knocked, but there had been no answer. Babe's plan now was to try the handle and see if it was unlocked. Yeah, like I said—breaking and entering.

"You go inside first, so when the police come, I can attest this was all your idea." I took a step back and the winter wind assaulted my already frozen skin. I ignored it. "In fact, maybe I'll just wait out here."

"Laura, people around here look out for one another. Look at her house. Something is not right."

I had to agree that her house was even more neglected than

usual. If I thought Candace had taken an unexpected trip and her home was empty, then vandals—or dare I say gangs, even?—might also notice and take advantage of the fact. I shivered at the thought of crime moving into the peaceful neighborhood.

Flashbacks of Chicago slammed into my mind. I touched the scar below my collar bone. The mark still throbbed a year later. Survivor's guilt, maybe? I closed my eyes as sweat sprinkled across my forehead. I could still feel the knife, the—

"Laura?"

I yanked my eyes open and saw Babe snapping her fingers mere inches in front of my face. I'm not in Chicago anymore. I'm in suburbia. Boring. Sweet—but safe—suburbia. Things like what had happened to me in Chicago didn't happen here.

Did they?

I could put my fears at ease simply by checking on my neighbor.

Babe's voice took on a sweet tone. "Come on, Laura. If you were out of town and your storm door was banging on its hinges, wouldn't you want me to check things out? Wouldn't you want me, or someone, to close it for you before the real bad guys realized you were out of town and stole all your valuables?"

The bad guys would be sorely disappointed if they tried to steal my valuables. The most they'd get was my DVD collection of *The Real Housewives*. My husband believed in living on a budget. A tight budget. A really tight budget. In my less-than-stellar moments, I might have even called him a penny pincher a time or two.

Babe tapped her foot. "Well?"

I considered what I'd want done if I were in Candace's shoes. Maybe we could just check out things inside her home and then lock the door behind us as we left. I had a lot to learn about this "being neighborly" thing. In Chicago, being neighborly just meant saying hello as you passed each other in the hallway of the apartment building. I might even go as far to say that in the big city, we practiced "mind your own business" as a way of showing we cared.

"Okay, but we check it out and then go. The last thing I need is the gossip girls telling everyone that I'm a criminal who moved to Boring to escape the law."

Babe smiled as if the idea amused her. She knew better than anyone how people in this town were prone to speculation. But her smile disappeared as she twisted the handle and the front door opened freely. "Anyone home? Candace? Jerry?"

We looked at each other. An unlocked front door wasn't good. Not good at all.

"Candace?" Babe called again.

Silence.

"They're not home." I jerked my thumb behind me. "Let's just go. I'll clean up the yard myself. Roll the trash cans back up the drive."

"Nonsense. We need to make sure everyone is okay."

She stepped inside and circled her hand in a "follow me" motion. I closed my eyes and imagined elderly Babe being clobbered by an intruder while I stood outside and waited for her. I sighed. "I'm coming."

I stepped onto the tiled foyer. Balls of dust danced across the floor as the wind swept into the room. I wasn't the world's best housekeeper, by any means, but smelling the inside of Candace's house made me vow to do better. It was a mixture of dirty socks, rotting trash, and something else I couldn't identify. Decaying meat, maybe?

"We'll just do a quick walk-through. Then we'll leave. I promise." She held up three fingers in what I assumed to be an attempt at Scout's honor.

That's when I heard someone in the distance. My heart stuttered, and I grabbed Babe's arm, pulled her back. "Do you hear that?" My own voice rose with each syllable and broke with a pubescent-sounding squeak. "Voices."

She nodded, a twinkle in her eyes. "We should be careful."

"How about 'we should leave'?"

She took another step forward and grinned, her eyes dancing. "I don't think she will hurt us."

I paused and listened to the tinny sound coming from near the steps. The TV. Of course. I could hear Oprah talking about how a new brand of jeans could flatter every woman's figure. That's what I needed: flatter, not fatter jeans. And I needed to mind my own business.

Tension knotted at my neck regardless. Storm door unlatched. Garbage cans on the street. Lawn ragged. Candace had time to watch TV but not to take care of her home? None of it sounded like the Candace I knew.

I crept forward, Babe in the lead. We passed the formal living room, which was loaded with boxes full of papers, videos, and magazines. I paused at the stairway and glanced up steps cluttered with shoes, clothes, magazines, and sheets of coupons. Coupons, for goodness sake? That's like newly found gold. I cocked my head and listened. The sound of the TV definitely came from the den. If the house turned out to be empty, we would click off the TV, lock the door, and leave. Our good deed of the day. I'd appreciate it if someone did the same for me.

"Just take a peek, Laura." Babe nodded toward the den. "In case."

"Why me?"

"Because I'm elderly."

Convenient. I shook my head and started down the short hallway, past the coat closet and into the den. I stopped abruptly, and she nearly trampled me.

Candace lay on the couch, eyes closed, mouth open. Her slender arms were neatly folded across her chest.

I looked at Babe. "Sleeping?"

My partner stepped back, one hand on her throat. "You check."

My eyes widened. "Babe! You're the one who insisted we do this."

She recovered somewhat and peered past me at the couch and Candace. "You first."

I chewed on my lip. I just wanted to put this whole experience behind me. I would apologize to Candace for interrupting her nap and then leave before any more damage could be done.

I took a step forward. "Candace?" No snoring. I stepped closer. The remote rested in one hand and a bag of pork rinds in the other. This wasn't like the Candace I knew. She hated that hulking flat screen hanging over the mantle. Her husband gave that TV more attention than he did his own wife.

Leaning down, I nudged her shoulder. Candace Flynn emitted a raspy hissing, like the exhalation of a tire going flat—or a corpse expelling gasses. That's when I recognized the source of the terrible stench.

Candace Flynn.

# 2

"So let me get this straight. That is the exact way you found her?" Chief Romeo—who looked anything but the name—stared at me like I'd positioned Candace on the couch as a joke. His caterpillar-like brows hung suspended on his forehead. His belly bounced up and down in cadence with his uncertain nod, and his pudgy fingers sprawled on his hips. We'd been at this for nearly an hour.

"That was the exact way we found her." I rubbed my arms against the winter breeze, not really minding the cold since it beat being inside my neighbor's house with a dead body any day. I glanced across the street and spotted two other neighbors, Donna and Tiara, staring at me like I was going to be crowned the new Gossip Queen soon.

"When was the last time you saw her?"

"She came over last Thursday after the monthly Homeowners' Association meeting." Candace had been going on and on about how evil Homeowners' Associations were. The negativity made me wonder why she bothered to act as treasurer of the organization.

I have to admit, after a few minutes, I'd tuned her out. Rachael Ray was coming on TV, and I didn't want to miss that episode of *30-Minute Meals*. Rachael had become an unofficial hero of mine. I'd never been the domestic type. Everyone knew me as a bona fide career woman, someone voted Most Likely to Succeed in high school. But since I currently didn't have a job, I was determined to learn how to cook. I never missed an episode of Rachael Ray.

I should have listened better to my friend that day. Who knew that would be one of the last times I'd talk to Candace?

An officer had led Babe to his squad car for questioning at the same time Chief Romeo pulled me aside, probably to see if our stories matched up. I glanced over at the vehicle and saw Babe's hands flying in the air. I'm sure Babe's version of the story sounded more interesting than mine. That was Babe for you. Spunky and animated. Me? I was the reliable, detailed one. But even with my level-headedness, my heart still squeezed in grief and tears threatened to spill over.

"Do you know where Mrs. Flynn's husband is?"

Jerry. Poor, poor Jerry. Even though he was a royal jerk most of the time, someone needed to call and tell him the news. I didn't wish the death of a loved one on anyone, however much of an insensitive clod he might be. "South Carolina. Golfing. He should be home in a couple of days."

Chief Romeo shifted and, I couldn't be certain, but the ground may have jolted with the motion. He jotted something else in his little notepad before glancing back at me. "Have you noticed any strange behavior on either of their parts?"

"Strange behavior?" I searched my mind. I'd only lived in Boring for nine months, and I was still trying to figure out what was strange and what was normal. "They were Trekkies."

"Trekkies?"

"Yeah, you know. They liked Star Trek. Went to conventions. Had costumes even." I'd classify that as strange.

Romeo sighed, pulled his lips back and exposed his teeth in what may have been a pensive, rankled expression. Instead of tuning into his possible exasperation, I tuned into his teeth. It appeared the town's dear officer of the law had been eating at the Pronto Café before being called out to the crime scene. How did I know? The restaurant's specialty was green eggs and ham. A big blob of green lay plastered next to his left incisor. I had to look away.

If Romeo was the face of the Boring Police Department, I didn't feel inspired to confidence. Luckily, the biggest crime here was the city folks' littering. At least, that's what the town troublemaker, Emma Jean, would say.

Until today. I swallowed. My stomach churned as Candace's pasty face flashed in my mind.

"Anything aside from the usual strange behavior?" Romeo asked.

I ran a hand through my bobbed hair, trying to review the

past week. Trying to make my head come back down to earth. "No, not that I can think of."

"Any enemies?"

"I'm the wrong person to ask. I've been here less than a year, and I know her, but not like most people around town would."

The lights from the patrol car flashed in the street, the fading sunlight brightening them. Other neighbors peered from their windows. Not Candace, though.

Candace would never snoop again.

I pinched myself, hoping to wake up and discover this was just a nightmare. God, please let me hear my alarm clock … and soon.

"Ma'am?" Romeo was staring at me.

"Yes?"

"Anything suspicious going on in the neighborhood?"

Last week I saw my neighbor Tiara, known by Babe as Miss Priss, buying motor oil at the General Store as though she was going to pop open the hood and work on her car herself. As if that was allowed by the Homeowners' Association. That was the epitome of suspicious behavior in Dullington Estates as of late. I mentally yawned.

"Not to my knowledge," I said.

He reached into his back pocket and produced a rumpled rectangle. "Here's my card. Give me a call if you think of anything."

Before I could respond, a beat up white Oldsmobile swerved into the cul-de-sac and skidded to a dramatic stop in front of the

Flynns' house. Harry McCoy stepped out. I rolled my eyes and caught Chief Romeo doing the same thing. Thirty-something Harry thrust his broad shoulders back. As he strode toward us, he tucked his khaki-colored shirt into his slim-cut matching pants. A few curls of dark hair escaped from the top of his shirt. Despite the winter breeze, Harry didn't wear a coat. Come to think of it, had I ever seen him in a coat? He probably thought himself too macho for something as inconsequential as warmth and comfort.

From what I'd heard—thanks to my recent involvement with the rumor mill—Harry wanted to be a part of the town's police force, only there were no openings. So what did he do? The next best thing—he headed up the Neighborhood Watch patrol. He took his position very seriously. When my husband locked himself out of the house and tried to crawl in through a window, Harry had pulled him back outside single-handedly. It was no small task, considering Kent weighed 200 pounds.

"I heard the siren and came right over." Harry's prominent chin jutted out as he gazed over the cul-de-sac, his domain. He looked at Chief Romeo. "So, what's going on?"

"I'm sorry, Harry." Chief Romeo shook his head, chewing as he did so. He must have found that leftover green egg. "This is official police business, nothing that the Neighborhood Watch needs to be involved with."

"I beg to differ." Harry spoke with slow precision. "I'm in charge of keeping this neighborhood safe. So why don't you fill me in?"

Chief Romeo sighed and shifted, the action causing his stomach to bounce like a water balloon. "Harry, I'm going to have to ask you to back off. You're not a part of police investigations. How many times have we been over this?"

Harry raised his hand in the air. "I've sworn to serve this community. And that's exactly what I intend on doing. I will not let my neighbors down here in Dullington Estates."

I stuffed Chief Romeo's card into my pocket and headed across the street. I'd heard enough of the conversation, and I knew I was no longer needed. I'd given my statement, and Chief Romeo would be in touch if he needed me.

Babe waved at me enthusiastically as I walked past the squad car. The poor officer sat with shoulders slumped, as if listening to Babe exhausted him.

I continued on home, desperate to get away from the crazy around me—which meant avoiding Donna and Tiara, despite their gossip-hungry eyes.

I still couldn't believe it. How could Candace be dead? How did she die? Was it an accident—did she choke on a pork rind? I certainly wouldn't guess that based on the position in which I'd found her. She'd looked too peaceful sprawled out on the couch.

That was it! Candace had looked too peaceful.

Like she'd been positioned on that sofa.

Which would mean someone killed her.

※※※

My eyes fluttered open. I lay on my couch.

I sprang forward, my gaze darting around for a remote and pork rinds. And Chief Romeo. And muscle-bound Harry. And crime scene tape. Anything else to tell me I'd died just like Candace.

What I saw was my house as my neighbors would see it, if they'd found me here dead on the couch. I'd rushed out earlier, knocking over a potted plant, and dirt still stretched across the hardwood floor. Laundry sat in piles on the loveseat. And who could ignore the dust that coated every available surface? I hadn't quite taken to house cleaning as my husband had hoped.

"Honey, are you okay?" Kent leaned over me.

I gasped and pressed my hand over my heart. Kent. He'd been sitting in a chair beside me. Just Kent. Not a killer.

How was I? I seemed to be alive. But I had to get off this couch. Maybe it was the couch that killed Candace. Maybe the furniture had taken on a mind of its own and—

No sooner had I stood than Kent propelled me back down. "You're not going anywhere."

I frowned. Kent didn't understand. Had we ever understood each other, or was understanding simply an act people perfected during dating and completely abandoned after marriage? "I don't want to die on the couch."

"You're not going to die on the couch, honey."

I stared into my husband's teddy-bear brown eyes. I loved those eyes. They were what first attracted me to him my sophomore year at Northwestern. His oval face had gotten fuller with age. I liked the change. He was too skinny when we got married. The fitness nut had run cross-country for our college and maintained his slim build, up until recently. Now he just looked normal.

"Then where?"

"Where what?"

"Where will I die?"

"You're not going to die. You're just traumatized. Babe caught me on the front walk and told me all about it. Give it time." He sat down in a ladder-back chair beside me. A football game cheered in the distance. The announcer proclaimed a touchdown.

"Yes!" I heard my loving husband say.

Glad he was so concerned about me that he couldn't enjoy the game.

Kent was mesmerized by the tube. He used to stare at me like that. Six years of marriage later, things had changed. It wasn't that we were unhappy. We were just—comfortable, I supposed.

"Kent?"

He turned toward me and picked up my hand with both of his. I pulled myself up slightly and rubbed my eyes, trying to recall the chain of events that had played out. They flashed back, all too vividly. Still, I found myself asking, "What happened?"

"Candace is dead, honey."

I bit back a sarcastic *really?* "I know. What happened to me?"

He patted my hand. "You just had a little panic attack. It's not unusual after something like you saw."

How long had I been out of commission? Were there any developments since then? "Have you heard anything about her? About what happened?"

He shook his head, and I noticed he needed a haircut. His brown hair touched the top of his ears. "No, sweetie. I don't think the police know anything yet."

"How about Babe? Is she okay?"

"Last I heard, she was trying to organize a press conference in her front lawn. Chief Romeo put the kibosh on that. Besides, Charlie Henderson would have been the only person there to ask questions." Charlie was the editor and reporter of the Boring Times.

What a contrast. In my former life, I'd worked in public relations. I'd been close to being named partner when Kent decided we should move. Kent said I should take it easy here before looking for another job—like there were any.

My smile only lasted a minute. I squeezed my eyes shut as flashes from today went off in my head. I tried to get the images out of my mind. I couldn't. I still saw Candace. I smelled the rotting trash needing to be taken out. I heard Oprah blaring in the background. I grasped Kent's hand more firmly.

"I found her." My throat burned as I said the words. Why had I let Babe talk me into going into that house? How much counseling would it take for me to recover from this?

"I know. It's going to take time for all of us to process what happened." He stroked my hair. "Especially you."

I sank back into the couch. I'd never get over the image of

her dead body lying there with the remote and pork rinds.

Nor would I get over the image of my husband watching football in the midst of my trauma.

# 3

"Jerry Flynn here. I'm also known around town as the Couch King. Come and see my furniture showcase." Dressed in tights, a tunic, an oversized crown, and a robe trimmed with faux fur, Jerry sprawled back onto his throne—a couch. "At the Couch King, we give all of our customers the royal treatment."

That commercial seemed to come on every fifteen minutes during the hours between breakfast and lunch. Jerry couldn't get enough of himself.

Speaking of the royal treatment, I had an unwanted visit to make in thirty minutes. At 11:00, to be exact. Hillary Kaye had summoned me by phone. Hillary was the president of the Homeowners' Association, and to say she ruled the neighborhood with an iron first would be an understatement. People feared standing up to the woman, afraid she'd slap a fine on them for some kind of infringement. Rumor had it that she even had the power to foreclose on a home if she saw fit.

So how would I get to her house today? Walk across Dullington Estates? Take the car in case a fast getaway proved needful? Nah. I would walk to her place. Sure, the weather remained frigid outside, but since moving to suburbia, I'd quickly learned that driving everywhere packed on the pounds. My hips proved it.

I'd walked everywhere in Chicago, and I liked it that way.

I sighed and clicked the TV off. Yes, Jerry preferred to be known around town as the Couch King, but everyone really called him the Couch Potato King. His contribution to his fledgling business was spending the entire budget on low-grade commercials. The rest of his time he stayed in his office and watched TV. Believe me, Candace had told me all about it—numerous times.

If Jerry was the Couch Potato King, his wife then became known as the Couch Potato's Wife. Of course, no one said that to her face. But believe me, things got around here in Boring, Indiana.

Poor Candace.

I couldn't stop thinking about her, about the way she'd been left dead.

Three days had passed since I found her. For as long as I could remember, I haven't even been able to look at bodies at funerals or viewings. The thought of stumbling upon a freshly-dead one still caused me to go cold. And the thought never strayed far from my mind. It always popped up at the worst times—actually, all the time.

Candace had been a force to be reckoned with. I hadn't completely figured her out, but there was something about her I liked. Once I got past her constant complaining, her negative demeanor, and overly-assertive personality, I saw Candace as someone who'd resigned herself to a life she didn't want. I'd been rooting for her to find a slice of happiness again. Maybe if she could, I could too.

I guess that wouldn't be happening. Maybe on either count?

Something banged in the distance. Someone was at the door. I left the living room window and pulled open the front door. There was Babe, wearing a Kiss Me, I'm Irish T-shirt that showed off the fat rolls at her stomach. A wide grin stretched across her glossy, pink lips.

"Hey, chickaroonie." She barged inside my house, and I could smell Philosophy, her favorite perfume. Hers and millions of twenty-somethings. "What's up with you? Haven't talked to you in a few days, so I wanted to get the nine-one-one. You know, gab, shoot the breeze, catch up a bit."

Four-one-one. It's four-one-one, Babe.

I followed her with my gaze, wondering how she managed to get inside so effortlessly like that. I gave up and closed the door behind me. "Nothing new here. And you?"

She shrugged. "I'm knitting."

"Knitting? That doesn't sound like you." It actually sounded like an activity someone her age would participate in. She always stayed far away from those things.

"What's old is new." She stopped at the doorway to my living room, placed a fist at her hips, and did a little shimmy that made me realize she'd been watching Shakira videos again. "Did you hear the latest?"

"The latest?"

"On Candace."

"No, I sure haven't." My pulse pounded at my ears. Boy, did I want to hear the latest. And Babe was just the person to tell me. She never disappointed.

"She was poisoned."

I touched my throat, feeling as if I'd just swallowed arsenic. "Poisoned? Are you sure?"

"That's what Romeo told Annie, who told Emma Jean, who told me. Annie and Romeo used to date, you see. He would like to date her again, so he tells her things he's mum about to other people in an effort to win her over. It'll never happen."

I leaned against the wall by my front door, unsure if I could move at the moment. "Tell me more."

"Annie just doesn't think that Romeo's her type—"

"About the murder, Babe."

"Oh. Well, they tested the pork rinds. Apparently, someone put ground up sleeping pills on them. Then they smothered Candace with something. She died peacefully, they said."

"So it was murder."

"Of course."

Of course. What else could it be here in the most peaceful little town in the Midwest? I swallowed the sarcasm. "Do they have suspects?"

"The husband is always a suspect."

Jerry. Could he have killed his wife? Sure, he was lazy. But a killer? Honestly, he was too lazy to think up a plan for murdering his wife. Maybe if the crime had been sloppy, he could be guilty. But something that would require careful planning, like poisoning pork rinds? No way. "I'm surprised he's not back from South Carolina yet."

"No one can find him."

I straightened. "No one can find him?"

"I guess Romeo called the resort where he was supposed to be staying, but they said he never showed up."

A million scenarios raced through my mind. Had someone killed Jerry as well? Was his body just waiting to be discovered somewhere? Would I be the one to trip over it too? I crossed my arms over my chest. How could this happen in safe little Boring, Indiana? In Chicago, I'd expect it. But not here.

"So, you wanna go do Zumba with me?" Babe grabbed her leg and attempted to pull it toward her chest. She nearly toppled over instead. I quickly grabbed her arm to steady her. She straightened with a "harrumph."

"Since when are you doing Zumba?" That would explain her earlier shimmy, I supposed.

"Since Karen Jones one street over started offering classes at her house." Babe leaned closer. "But don't tell Hillary. I'm sure it's a violation of the Homeowners' Association somehow."

"Speaking of Hillary," I glanced at my watch. "She called and asked if I could meet with her today. Something about doing damage control in the neighborhood after Candace—you know." The image appeared again, and I shook my head to dislodge it.

Babe walked toward the door, jabbing me with her knuckles as she passed. That woman had strength for her age. "Okay, chickaroonie. Take care of yourself."

And as quickly as Babe had appeared, she was gone.

I only had twenty minutes before meeting Hillary, so I'd better get going. Hillary despised tardiness. At our monthly Homeowners' Association meetings, she locked the door precisely when the meeting started so no latecomers could get in.

Yet, she wanted more people to participate.

The woman had her opinions, for sure. Her methods, well, those were another story. She and Candace could have had a tight competition over who held the "Most Despised" title in the neighborhood.

I wrapped a colorful scarf around my neck, pulled a stocking cap over my hair, and shut the door behind me.

The last time I'd seen Hillary had been at one of the Homeowners' Association meetings. I went only because I had nothing better to do than torture myself. Very few things qualified as worse than sitting through a meeting detailing all the many rules of the neighborhood. The best part—we paid a monthly fee for someone else to tell us how we could keep up our house. No basketball hoops out front, no changing the oil on our property, no above-ground pools in the backyard. Excessive, if you asked me. But you signed a contract when you moved into the neighborhood, vowing you'd obey the rules and regulations. Of course, it was only after you moved in that you realized exactly what all the rules were. By then, you'd signed your life away and it was too late. They had you.

Not even fifteen minutes later, I walked up the sidewalk to Hillary's perfectly manicured property. Even in the winter the lawn appeared green and lush. The flowerbeds still had a touch of color to them. The bushes were neat and trimmed. How did she do it? She had three kids to keep her busy. I couldn't keep up my lawn and I didn't even have a dog.

Hillary greeted me at the door with her normal plastic smile and icy blue eyes. "You're punctual. Good. We have a lot to discuss."

The slim blonde ushered me inside her ultra-clean house. Her home reminded me of Hillary—not beautiful, but neat and attractive with everything in order. She walked briskly to the camel-back couch and perched on the cushion's edge. With precision, she draped her hands over her knees and looked at me like I was her first-round draft pick.

Did I just use a football analogy? I'd better be careful, or I'd be tempted to join Kent in watching guys dressed in tights chase a ball across the field.

"I'm really worried about how Candace's death will affect everyone in Dullington Estates. I'm hoping you have ideas on how we can be proactive and head off a disaster."

I lowered myself into a chair across from her, feeling as tense as Hillary looked.

"Disaster?" Was I missing something? Had For Sale signs appeared up and down the street overnight? Were middle-class white collar workers suddenly forming street gangs?

Her gaze was so sharp that prickles shivered up my arms. "A murder in the neighborhood is the worst thing that could happen here. I try to see to it that everyone in the association is safe, that we don't succumb to the lures of other neighborhoods that are riddled with crime and bad lawn ornaments."

"Of course." I resisted a smirk.

"So, how can we assure people that they're safe? Do you have any ideas?"

I shifted in my seat and tried to find the right words. "Are people safe? I mean, a killer is out there somewhere. We don't want to give people false security."

Hillary twitched like I'd just thrown ice water on her face. "Of course they're safe. This wasn't the work of a psycho killer who picks random victims."

I cleared my throat, realizing I needed to tread carefully. I had to draw on all of my experience with office politics and dealing with difficult people. Basically, I had to become plastic also. "Am I missing something? I mean, how do you know that for sure? You have to be pretty psycho to kill someone."

"I will maintain the dignity of this neighborhood, with or without your help!" Hillary's nostrils flared and her eyes lit with fire.

So much for drawing on my skills in office politics.

I held my hands up. "Okay, okay. I'll help in whatever way I can. But, above all, we have to be honest."

We decided on an impromptu meeting the next evening where Harry would talk to residents about how to keep their homes safe. The idea seemed to satisfy Hillary. I was sure it would make Harry's day, too.

As I walked home, I actually enjoyed the sharp breeze that slapped my face. It beat talking to Hillary any day. Perhaps she was right—maybe Candace's murder had been the work of someone close to her. Maybe there was nothing else for the rest of us to worry about. I sure hoped so.

My mailbox hung open. The mailman usually didn't come until later in the day, so he must have gotten a head start this morning. I crossed the street and reached inside the glossy black box. A single white envelope waited inside with my name scribbled across the front. No stamp, no address. Just my name. Weird… and a little creepy.

Perhaps it was a note from a neighbor, requesting that we add more mulch to our flowerbeds or trim our bushes. People on this street tended to be picky about these things. Mostly about Candace's home and its upkeep. I bit down on my lip. Candace wasn't alive anymore for people to send these notes to or for people to threaten to turn her in to the association.

I shrugged it off and ripped the envelope open as I walked toward my front door. A single sheet of paper with a typed message was enclosed. I paused on my porch and braced myself for whatever complaint I was about to face.

My bones froze. Not from the weather, but from a cooler

chill—one that started inside. I read the note again.

*One murder makes people worry, then how about two? Who'll be the next victim, will it be you? Keep your eyes open and watch what you eat, tell anyone you got this and you'll be under six feet. Don't even tell your husband, who may know too much, or murder number three may happen as such.*

*I'm watching you, Laura Berry.*

I looked around the street for a suspicious face. No one. Not even a car driving by.

I slipped the letter back into the envelope and cast one more glance around the cul-de-sac.

I made a promise to myself a year ago, and that pledge was to never be a victim again.

I raised my head, in case anyone was watching from an unseen place. I wouldn't show my fear. Wouldn't be weak.

Bring it, psycho. Because when you try, I'm going to catch you red-handed.

# 4

Despite my earlier bravado, I couldn't ignore the tremble that shook me for the rest of the day. I nestled onto the couch and tried breathing exercises before Kent got home so he wouldn't see my fear and ask about it. After all, the note said I couldn't tell anyone, especially not Kent. But how exactly would someone know if I did tell him?

That led me to one conclusion and one conclusion only. Whoever had sent that note was not only a psychopath, but stupid.

However, psycho and stupid were still good reasons for me to tremble.

The front door opened. I checked the time. Eight p.m. Another long day. With each long day was the chasm in our marriage becoming wider and deeper? I hoped not.

"Look what I found on the porch."

I turned around, clueless as to what he was talking about. My eyes widened when I spotted a bag of pork rinds and a DVD. I dove across the room and slapped both objects from his hands.

"What are you doing?" Kent stared at me like I'd grown two horns and a pointy tail.

"Pork rinds?" I raised my hands in the air and felt my nostrils flaring. Did I have to spell it out for him?

Realization washed over his face. "Candace."

"Yeah. Death by pork rinds. Not a good way to go, in my opinion."

"It wasn't the pork rinds that killed—" He paused and shook his head.

That was Kent. Always logical. Even at times when logic had no place—like times when my emotions could dropkick his reasoning and take it out in two seconds flat.

His gaze stopped on something on the floor. "What's with the DVD?"

My throat went dry as I thought about it. "Should we see?"

"I suppose we should. Maybe this is just a twisted misunderstanding."

"Twisted misunderstanding. Of course."

Only my husband would think that. Normal husbands would be pulling out shotguns. Okay, at the very least they'd be calling out someone to install a home alarm system.

We walked toward the DVD player. Each step caused my heart to race. Kent seemed as calm as the lake behind our house on a windless day as he slipped in the disc. I sat back on the couch, trying to appear nonchalant. But my fingers gave me away. They wouldn't stay still. They twisted and picked at hangnails, and my knuckles suddenly needed to be cracked.

A grainy picture came on our TV screen. I squinted, trying to determine what I was watching.

That's when I realized I was watching me.

"What...?" Kent's face wrinkled with concern and he leaned closer to the screen.

I couldn't take my eyes off the TV. Sure enough, there I was, climbing into my SUV. When was that recorded? The video jumped in time and showed me pulling into the driveway. I walked to the back of my SUV and pulled out several bags of groceries.

Two days ago. That's when I'd gone grocery shopping.

Someone had videotaped me coming and going, and I'd been clueless.

Even more disturbing? Based on the camera angle, whoever had videotaped me seemed to be positioned inside the Flynns' house.

"I don't like this. I don't like it at all." Kent and I looked at each other before he shook his head and picked up the phone. "I'm calling the police."

※※※

The next day, bags hung deep under my eyes. A night of contemplating who'd been watching you and videotaping you and was now threatening you for unknown reasons could do that to a girl. Chief Romeo's promise last night to look into the mysterious DVD brought me little comfort.

After drinking four cups of coffee, I felt a little better. More awake, at least.

Just as I turned the shower on to get ready for the day, the doorbell rang. Probably Babe. Being neighborly, no doubt. I turned the water off. Conversations with Babe could take awhile.

So, with my hair flying out from the clip holding it back from my face and my faded pink bathrobe wrapped around me in the most unflattering way, I opened the door.

There stood Donna and Tiara, grinning with their picture-perfect hair and makeup. Did these two ever not look put together and camera ready? I'd been like that when I worked a nine-to-five job, but now that my main job was scrubbing toilets, sweats and T-shirts would do.

I pulled my bathrobe tighter and forced a smile. "Good morning."

"I hope we didn't catch you at a bad time." Donna extended a basket of muffins. "I thought a few homemade goodies might cheer you up."

That was Donna for you—always proper, polite and the perfect housewife. With her petite features and striking auburn hair, she was the essence of a suburban socialite.

"Thanks. That's kind of you."

"We wanted to check and see how you were doing," Tiara offered. She stood nearly six feet tall, willowy, and had strong features that made me wonder if she'd been a model in her younger days. Her hair was cut stylishly short, and her ebony skin was flawless. "That was quite a scare you had."

I realized I was being rude by not inviting them inside out of the cold. Hesitantly, I stepped back and extended my arm. "Please, come in."

Usually, people who cared too much about appearances annoyed me, but Donna and Tiara were the neighborhood equivalent of the cool crowd in high school. If you got in with them, you had an instant circle of friends. I could use friends right now. I mean, sure, I had Babe. I loved Babe. But I could use other friends as well. And Donna and Tiara were beginning to see me in too many less-than-stellar moments.

My neighbors trotted inside, shoving the muffins in my hands as they passed.

"Would you like some coffee? Tea?" I asked, closing the front door and the only hope of maintaining my dignity.

"I would love coffee. Do you mind?" Tiara asked.

Donna smiled sweetly. "Me too."

I'd just started brewing another pot. I got down two mugs and filled them to my neighbor's specifications. I glanced at the muffins and reached for one. My hand froze mid-air. What if they were poisoned? I didn't want to think the worst of my two neighbors, but I didn't know whom I could trust. After a moment of contemplation, I grabbed a tray and loaded it up with the coffee and then placed the muffins there. I would wait for one of them to eat one before I did.

This would be the reality of my life until the killer was behind bars.

I forced a smile as I hurried back into the living room. The two ladies stopped whispering when I walked into the room and my self-consciousness soared. I knew they had been gossiping, I just didn't know who their subject of the day was. Most likely me.

I tucked a hair behind my ear and set my coffee onto a side table. "Everything okay with both of you lately?"

They nodded in sync.

"We really just wanted to check on you." Tiara took a sip of her coffee, her big eyes peering over the rim of the mug. They'd both passed on the muffins. That meant I did, too. I'd toss them into the trash after my neighbors left. "How are you doing, sweetie?"

I remembered the note in my mailbox—how could I forget?—and inwardly grimaced. Again, I couldn't speak of the threat. I didn't know whom I could trust with the information. "I can't stop thinking about Candace."

"Me either." Tiara nodded vigorously. "I mean, who would have done something like that to her?"

I shrugged. "Good question."

"People have all kinds of theories," Donna chimed in. "It seems like everyone in town is a suspect." Donna glanced at Tiara. "I mean, not us, of course."

"Like whom? Who's a suspect?"

Tiara and Donna looked at each other, as if they had to at least try and appear hesitant about spreading gossip. Finally, Tiara cleared her throat. When she met my gaze, I saw a twinkle in her eyes that exposed her excitement. "The word is the police brought Babe in for questioning this morning."

I nearly spit out my coffee. "Babe? That's ridiculous."

Donna nodded quickly. "She takes sleeping pills. That's what the police found on the pork rinds. Someone sedated Candace and then ..."

She didn't need to finish the sentence. "I'm sure a lot of people take sleeping pills." No way did Babe kill Candace. No way. For goodness sake, I had sleeping pills! I hadn't taken them in a year, but I had them, just in case the nightmares came back. "Besides, why would Babe want Candace dead? She has no motive."

"Babe's a little—" Tiara twirled her index finger around her ear in the universal sign for "loopy."

I had to defend my spunky neighbor, the first person who'd befriended me when I moved here. "She's not loopy in a crazy way. She's just different. She's not afraid to be herself. I wish I had more of her gumption."

Donna leaned forward, coffee perched in her hands. "Who do you think did it, Laura? Do you have any theories? I mean, you were the one who found her dead."

I sat back. As much as I'd thought about it, I didn't really have any ideas. I wish I did.

"It seems like everyone had a problem with Candace in one way or another," I said.

"That's for sure." Tiara nodded.

I leaned forward. "How about the two of you? Did you ever

get mad at her?"

Donna's coffee slipped from her grasp and shattered all over the wood floor.

"Oh dear!" She rushed to her feet and stared at the mess. "What have I done?"

I sprang into action, guilt assaulting me that I'd made her uncomfortable enough to react like this. "It's no problem, Donna. Those mugs were old anyway. Let me just get some paper towels."

"I don't know why I'm so clumsy lately."

I rushed into the kitchen and grabbed the whole roll.

I returned in time to see Tiara pat Donna's back. "You've been under a lot of stress lately, honey. Anyone in your situation would be jittery."

What was Donna stressed out about? I wondered. Maybe trying to balance her blended family: two teenagers of her own, and two stepchildren.

Or was she stressed out because she murdered Candace? She did live right next door, and our mailboxes were side by side. She could have easily slipped the note inside my box without anyone noticing.

I shoved the thought aside and began soaking up coffee. Donna kneeled to help, but I shooed her back to the couch. "Don't worry about it. Besides, I don't want you to stain your khakis."

"You're such a sweetie, Laura. I'm sorry you're mixed up in this whole mess."

I stopped sloshing the paper towels from the floor. "What do you mean?"

"We all know that it wasn't your idea to go into Candace's house. Babe coerced you, probably to make you look guilty and take the blame off of herself."

"Babe didn't kill Candace," I repeated, making a mound of wet paper towels on the floor. "The idea is ridiculous."

Tiara shrugged in a way that clearly stated she thought I was wrong. "Here, let me throw those away for you, sweetie. Then we've really got to be going." She swooped up the paper towels and went into my kitchen before I could object.

Donna reached into her purse and handed a plastic package to me. "Magic Wipes. They clean up anything. Keep the whole package. It's the least I can do."

After I took the wipes, she and Tiara looped arms.

"Let us know if we can do anything for you," Donna said.

"Of course." I stood and saw two brown blotches on my robe. Great. I wouldn't be winning any "most put together" contests. "Thanks for the muffins."

"We'll see you tonight at the association meeting." Tiara tinkled her manicured fingertips in the air.

That was right. The meeting was tonight. I'd almost forgotten in all of the craziness.

Who knew what kind of speculation I'd hear there.

Maybe enough to figure out who'd sent me that threatening note.

# 5

"The best advice I can give everyone here tonight is to lock your doors, don't eat pork rinds, and report any suspicious behavior." Harry stood at the podium on the stage of the aptly named Boring High School, and nodded repeatedly to the large turnout of concerned citizens seated in the hard wooden seats. Harry appeared to be trying to make eye contact with everyone at the association meeting to drive home his point. His over-the-top antics were enough to make me want to burst out laughing. I didn't, of course, because death was no laughing matter.

But with safety tips like those, I could have stayed home and still been all the wiser. Organizing my sock drawer seemed more appealing than this waste of time.

Besides, I could very well be the next corpse found here in the 'burbs. Someone wanted me either dead or quiet, and to keep me quiet I'd probably have to be dead. My odds weren't looking good.

Awkward silence fell over the auditorium. Finally, Hillary stood from her seat at the side of the stage, made her way to the podium, and cleared her throat.

Come on, Hillary. Don't do it. Don't show your prickly side.

"Thank you, Harry, for that groundbreaking advice." Her cheeks reddened.

The start of a smile tugged at my lips. On second thought, this was much more entertaining than organizing my sock drawer. These were the kind of uncomfortable moments that were usually reserved for reality TV.

Hillary tugged at the collar of her navy blue suit. "Does anyone have any questions?"

The silence did a 180. Suddenly, everyone began talking at once as hands shot in the air.

"Do the police know who did this?"

"How did Candace die?"

"Does anyone know where Jerry is?"

"Are we really safe?"

Hillary held up her hands. "One at a time, please!"

It was a moment for the history books. Hillary was losing her precious control. Kent and I looked at each other and grinned. That was one thing I had to give Hillary credit for: Our mutual disdain for her had pulled us closer together.

"Do the police have any suspects? Probably a city slicker," Emma Jean theorized. Emma Jean's family went back a hundred years in this town. For Emma Jean, newcomers weren't welcome in sweet little Boring. We were corrupt—and, as she often liked to say, litterers."

Harry shook his head. "The police aren't sharing any theories as to who they feel is guilty. But they do assure me that they're on top of this investigation."

More than likely, they'd told him to mind his own business.

"Are we safe? I mean, really safe, because I haven't been sleeping at night, I'm so worried that someone's going to get me too!" Tiara knitted her eyebrows together, looking much younger than her thirty-eight years.

Harry pushed his chest out further, and the Neighborhood Watch emblem on his knit shirt caught my attention. He must have a closetful of those shirts, one for each day of the week. "We can't live in fear. We have to resume our normal lives. After all, there's no evidence that would lead authorities to think that this is the work of a serial killer."

"A serial killer!" Pandemonium exploded again

Hillary's face turned red, and her eyes shot daggers at Harry. "I'm sure this was a crime of association. Nobody has anything to worry about!"

"How can you be sure? Did the police tell you that?"

"I've got children to think about! Speculation just isn't good enough."

"I moved here because it was supposed to be safe."

Hillary looked speechless. The gavel dangled in her hands, and her bottom lip dropped slightly.

An idea struck. Before I lost courage, I stood up and rubbed my hands on my slacks. "I have an idea, everyone."

Silence. All eyes zeroed in on me.

I swallowed and glanced quickly at Kent, who stared at me with wide, questioning eyes. I turned my gaze back to the crowd around me. "Why don't we add more people to our Neighborhood Watch program? Harry does a great job, but it's really too much work for just one person. We need to have a constant patrol, someone who can be on the lookout for anything out of the ordinary."

Noise erupted.

"Great idea."

"Let's do it."

"It's the perfect solution."

I could tell by looking at Harry that I'd just stepped on his toes. The Neighborhood Watch was his territory. I waited for his reaction. With the entire association around me, he couldn't throw much of a temper tantrum.

He nodded slowly, and his gaze never left me. It was as if he tried to send me a silent message, and I got it loud and clear: He did not appreciate my suggestion.

Finally, he said, "I guess it couldn't hurt to expand the program—at least until this killer is behind bars. The problem is, who's going to help? Everyone here has families, or they work full-time."

I slowly brought my hand up. "I will."

I felt Kent's sharp gaze on me.

"I mean, I'm not working right now. It makes sense that I should help."

"You have no experience with something like this!" Kent whispered. "It could be dangerous being out there by yourself."

Babe stood. "I'll help her. We can be partners." She grinned widely at me.

I couldn't help but smile back, even though the thought of working with Babe was enough to make my blood pressure skyrocket. Babe was likely to find trouble and jump into the middle of it instead of calmly calling the authorities.

Besides, wasn't she a suspect? I needed to talk to her later about her questioning down at police headquarters.

Harry shook his head. "Two women doing Neighborhood Watch? I don't know if that's such a good idea. Aren't there any men who can volunteer?" He looked back to the crowd.

"A woman can do this job just as well as a man!" Hillary cried. "I resent that comment, Harry."

He held up his hands in protest. "All right, all right. I guess since there'd be two of you, I'd feel better about it." Harry stared at us, his brows furrowed in thought. "I'll have to train you. This isn't a position for the weak."

Babe held up those three fingers again. "Weak isn't in my vocabulary."

Everyone looked at me.

"And I'm a city slicker. You know how we are."

Everyone nodded, as if that response satisfied them.

Hillary slammed her gavel onto her podium. "It's settled then. Laura and Babe will join our Neighborhood Watch. We'll have someone on duty at all times. This neighborhood will be safe!"

"Neighborhood Watch, huh?" Kent ran the razor down his cheek, plowing a puff of shaving cream, after we returned home from the meeting. He couldn't stand to go to bed with prickles on his face. It was one of his little quirks. "You never fail to surprise me. I never thought you'd be interested in something like that."

I sat in bed and continued to rub lotion over my hands. "I just want to do my part to contribute to the community. I think it will go a long way as far as establishing trust. Don't you?"

His eyebrows went up as he considered it. He moved the razor under his nose. "You're probably right. I just worry about you. There is a killer out there. And someone did leave pork rinds on our porch, not to mention that creepy DVD."

I shrugged, trying to appear nonchalant. In reality, this was the perfect excuse to get involved in this case. I had to find out who was threatening my husband and me before we both ended up six feet under.

"I'll just be doing patrol. I have no intention of tracking down any killers or taking the law into my own hands. I'm not Harry." My throat burned as the words left my lips. I didn't lie to Kent. Until today. But I couldn't tell him about the note. What if—just what if—whoever wrote that note was not only videotaping me, but also monitoring my conversations? I felt like a loon even thinking the thought. But right now I knew that the killer was three things: psycho, stupid, and technologically-savvy.

"It's not you I'm worried about. It's Babe. The woman has no fear."

I couldn't argue. Apparently the police had questioned her for three hours. Did she fret? Of course not. She enjoyed telling everyone, detail by detail, how the police had practically tortured her to get information. It had been worse than the interrogation methods at Guantanamo Bay, only they didn't use water torture. Instead, they used the good cop/bad cop routine.

Apparently, Babe's fingerprints had been found on the bag of pork rinds. She claimed she contemplated buying them at the General Store last week, then proceeded to telling an agonizingly long story about how she put them in her shopping cart, then put them back on the shelf, and repeated the process numerous times before deciding on Funyuns instead. Sadly, I believed her.

Kent climbed in bed beside me and turned on the TV. The theme song from CSI blared into the room. Using the remote, he set the timer for an hour before placing the controls back onto the nightstand. He kissed my forehead. "Goodnight, honey."

I bit back a frown. "Good night."

Next thing, we'd have Lucy and Ricky Ricardo beds.

Our marriage was not going according to the script I'd envisioned. I'd dreamed of being *Hart to Hart*. Instead, we were turning into that couple from the sitcom *Mad About You*—you know, the one about the crazy-in-love couple who almost gets divorced at the end of the series?

My mom had always warned me that my storybook fantasies would only disappoint me. I'd grown up watching too many

Disney movies and reading too many fairytales. Marriage wasn't like that.

My self-talk did nothing to lift to my spirits.

I had to think about something else. Candace seemed a good option.

I turned over in bed, trying to get comfortable. What had happened to my friend? Who could have killed her? Someone I knew? I couldn't stop considering the possibilities. It could have been anyone: one of my neighbors, someone I went to church with, a respected member of the community. The possibilities were endless.

And what did dear, sweet Kent know about it?

There my thoughts went back to Kent. We used to not have any secrets. Maybe that was our problem now—we both had too many secrets, too many separate interests. Would one of those secrets end up killing us?

I sighed, and tuned out the sound of the television.

Kent was right. This whole investigation was none of my business.

※※※

Of course it was my business. Candace was my friend. I was nothing if not loyal.

That was the conclusion I'd come to by the next morning. I'd tried to ignore my obsession with my neighbor's murder. Really. But I had a new reason to wake up each morning now in suburbia: murder.

As morbid as that sounded, I'd accept that reality in my life. It beat the other alternatives—that I was bored to death or clinically depressed.

That morning, for example, I had cleaned the floors, dusted the entire house, and reorganized the bathroom closet—an obvious sign of desperation. I moved one step beyond desperation and into insanity when the highlight of my hour was walking around the house while balancing five folded towels on my head. Being a housewife just wasn't my gig.

But solving a murder and saving my marriage just might be.

I was walking to my home office to retrieve a pen and paper—to write out a list of suspects—when I heard a loud thud in the backyard.

I froze in the hallway, and placed my hand on the wall to brace myself. Had I been hearing things? What was that sound? Someone trying to break into my house? Someone planting evidence to make Kent look guilty? Or maybe someone trying to hide bugs so they could hear if I ratted them out about the note?

I waited, holding my breath, because apparently my breathing's so deafening I might miss a loud—

Bang!

I threw myself into the wall. My heart raced.

The sound definitely came from my backyard. It wasn't crisp enough to be a gun, or concise enough to be a hammer.

Maybe someone was trying to break into my house to put some—bam!—on my food. Maybe that unlocked door the other day wasn't a coincidence in the least. After all, I was obsessive about locking all my doors and windows. I'd lived in downtown Chicago, for goodness sakes!

Okay, I had to think with a clear head. I needed to call the police. I needed to protect myself from whatever evil lurked outside my doors.

Where was the phone? I'd been carrying around the cordless earlier when my mother had called from Cincinnati. Of course I hadn't left it on the charger. That would make my life too easy.

I mentally retraced my steps. I thought I'd left it in my bedroom.

I slowly took a step, still clinging to the wall. Once I got to the doorway, I dropped to my knees, just in case anyone could see me through the window. I didn't want to be an easy target.

Two bangs sounded from outside. My heart raced.

I scrambled toward the bed and grabbed the phone. My fingers paused on the buttons.

Laura, think clearly. It could be neighbors in their backyard. Maybe it just sounds like your backyard.

Get a grip!

I needed to peek outside and make sure something suspicious was going on before I called the police. The noise sounded close. My gut told me so, and I had to trust my instincts.

I took a deep breath and crawled out of my bedroom, slid down the stairs, and crept into the living room, where the windows faced the backyard. Usually I enjoyed looking out those windows onto the deck. Behind the deck and the semi-green grass sparkled the retention pond—or lake, as others in the neighborhood liked to call it. A fountain spouted in the center, and ducks dotted the blue water. I caught glimpses of the golf course beyond the lake.

Today, the lake didn't matter, nor did my deck or the oh-so-popular golf course.

I only cared about the sound. Like a kid at a fun house who feared someone jumping out from behind a corner, I approached the window. I darted to the wall, pressing my back against it. Great, I'd turned from a kid at a funhouse into a James Bond wannabe.

I decided on the count of three, I'd move the curtain and glance outside. The action would be swift and stealth-like, so that if anyone outside were watching, he wouldn't even notice it. After all, I was a part of Neighborhood Watch. I could handle this.

My hands trembled as I reached for the drapes. I recited jargon I'd learned in the stress management classes I'd had to take when I worked for the PR firm. Focus your breathing. Visualize your goal. Maximize the moment.

The recitations weren't effective with my PR work, nor were they much use in life-threatening situations.

I moved the drape an inch and angled myself to take a peek. Sunlight streamed through, and I saw the edge of my new lawn furniture. The sun reflected on the lake.

Another bang ricocheted through my backyard.

The noise sounded close. My gut told me so, and, as an official member of the neighborhood law enforcement crew, I had to trust my instincts.

Just then, I heard someone turn the knob at the back door.

# 6

"Laura, I can't get into your shed!" Someone pounded at my backdoor hard enough to make my whole house shake. "Laura, I know you're there. I haven't seen you leave your house today."

Babe? Babe was making all of that noise?

I was going to kill her.

Maybe "kill" wasn't the best word choice when I considered the events of the past few days. I let my head fall back against the wall and laughed halfheartedly—it was either laugh or scream. Babe. Of course.

"Laura? It's cold out here. Are you trying to give an old woman pneumonia?"

"Coming!" I hurried across the room to the French doors off of the kitchen, and threw them open. "Babe, what are you doing? You scared me to death."

"I just need to trim my bushes, and I can't find my hedgers. I was hoping to borrow yours, but I can't get your shed open."

"That's because we put a lock on it."

"Now why would you go and do that? How am I supposed to get in now?"

Exactly.

"I'll get the hedgers for you, Babe. All you have to do is ask."

"I didn't want to bother you."

"Well, you scared me. I nearly called the police. There's a killer out there, Babe!"

"Flash!" Her fingers sprouted in the air and she looked at me with a "duh" expression.

I had no idea what she was trying to convey. "What?" I could hear the exasperation in my voice.

"You know, as in news flash."

I shook my head, still clueless.

"Okay, how about this one? 'Hello, Captain Obvious.'"

I put my hand on my hip. "I see. You're insulting me."

"Flash!" She grinned, proud of herself.

I narrowed my eyes, but before I could retort, Babe's eyes lit up.

"Hey, speaking of killers. Have you heard anything about Candace's funeral?"

Now that she mentioned it, I sure hadn't. And though I didn't want to let the subject of Babe insulting my intelligence to drop quite yet, I decided maybe it was best. Otherwise, I might be arrested for assaulting someone.

"No. I wonder who's planning it." Jerry and Candace didn't have any children. "Her parents?"

Babe shook her head. "They're both deceased."

"Brothers or sisters?"

"She's an only child."

I crossed my arms. "Well, the woman's got to have a funeral. Who would plan one in a case like this?"

"Jerry, I suppose."

"But he's missing. And maybe a killer."

"Now you're thinking like a member of the Neighborhood Watch, chickaroonie." Babe knuckled me on the chin. "I'm so proud."

"Maybe we should go to The Couch King. Maybe someone there knows something. I mean, it's been five days since we found her body. The woman needs a funeral!" I'd been thinking about visiting the store all day. This would be the perfect excuse. Not to get a couch, of course. To find out information.

"Just let me get my purse!"

Babe reappeared five minutes later. We climbed into my SUV and started down the road to The Couch King. I'd never been in the store myself, but I'd seen it enough times on television. I couldn't be sure, but I think Candace was offended that Kent and I insisted on shopping for furniture up in Indy. I didn't like to mix business with pleasure. It always ended up a disaster.

I pulled into a parking space outside the wooden building, which sat alone on a stretch of country road. Why Jerry had chosen this location for his business remained a mystery to me. The only people who ever passed this way were farmers or people traveling the back roads to Ohio. I supposed they needed furniture too, but still, hadn't Jerry ever heard the saying, "Location, location, location"?

"They should've used part of that advertising budget to fix up the place, huh?" Babe glanced back and forth from the building to me.

I stared at The Couch King. The store was nothing fancy, just an old storefront with big glass windows all along the front and a rugged wooden overhang that reminded me of the Old West. A cement slab served as the welcome mat, and I noticed the trim work on the building needed a fresh coat of paint. The mocha brown was peeling.

"You can say that again," I agreed.

Babe examined her bubble-gum pink fingernails. "You know rumors were flying that this business was about to go bust."

"Really?"

"Really. I mean, everyone knows that Jerry wasn't much of a businessman."

Had Jerry killed Candace in hopes of collecting a life insurance policy? It happened all the time in movies. But was Jerry really that smart? I'd have to think about it before suggesting the theory to Babe, who was likely to throw some teenage slang on me again if she didn't agree.

We hopped out and approached the front door. A little bell chimed as we walked inside. A woman with big hair and small clothes greeted us with a lipstick-on-the-teeth smile.

"Welcome to the Couch King. I'm Yvonne. Is there anything in particular you're looking for?"

I gripped my purse. I hadn't thought this far ahead. "I, uh, I'm looking for a—"

"I'm interested in a new couch." Babe plopped onto a puffy leather sofa and crossed her legs. "Maybe something formal."

"We've got plenty of those! Let me show you our selection. Any particular color?"

"What color do you think, Laura? You've got great taste." Babe stared at me with wide eyes.

Color? What color? I fixated on the lipstick on the sales woman's teeth. "Coral."

"Follow me." She curved her finger and wiggled it, instructing me to hurry along.

Couches were situated every which way, in no particular order. There wasn't even a distinct walkway. I dodged sofas—big ones, small ones, leather ones, floral ones. The floor inside matched the floor outside: cement. I could really give them a few marketing tips.

"I'm going to use the bathroom," Babe announced. "Laura will tell you what I want."

Babe slipped away toward the back and I stared at her retreating figure, trying to keep my mouth closed. How did Babe always manage to leave at the most convenient times—convenient for her, that is, and totally inconvenient for me?

"You new in town?" Yvonne asked, glancing back over her shoulder.

I double-timed a few steps to catch up with her. "As a matter of fact, yes, I am."

"It's a great place. I just love Boring. I don't actually live in town. I live up in Indy. Small towns are just a little too close-knit for me, if you know what I mean. But I love to visit them!"

I wanted to jump in with questions, but I held back. I needed to ease into the subject of Jerry's disappearance.

"Have you worked here long?"

"Twelve years."

I nearly choked on my saliva. "Twelve years? Wow. You really must like it."

"The owner's been really good to me."

Was this my opening? I opened my mouth to pose my next question, when the woman squealed.

"Isn't this couch just beautiful?" She fell backward onto the ugliest couch I've ever laid eyes on. It was coral, all right. Coral and big and lacy. A mix of retro and Victorian, clean lines and ruffles.

"Wow," I nodded, trying to find the words. "That is some couch."

"I just knew you'd love it. We're running a special this week. No interest for a year." Her arm stretched across the back and her eyes sparkled. "So, what do you say?"

"I'm sorry to hear about the owner's wife." Okay, I needed to practice my timing a little. But it was already said and out there. There was no taking it back. I held my breath and waited for her response.

The woman's eyes lost their sparkle. "Candace? I know. It's such a shame."

"How's Jerry doing?"

The woman's face suddenly became drawn. "Hard to say—he's out of town."

"The poor man must be in distress, to lose his wife like that. I can't imagine." I shook my head. I meant it. I couldn't imagine what Jerry would feel when he heard the news. Losing a wife because someone killed her? Did a soul ever recover from that?

I guess it did if you were the one who killed her.

"Their marriage had been in trouble for years." She raised her head, as if realizing how insensitive she sounded. "But yes, I'm sure this must be terrible for him."

"Has anyone here talked to him? When's he coming back? The funeral is probably soon, right?" Chill out, Laura. Go easy on the questions. I attempted to relax my shoulders. I was no good at this detective thing.

"I haven't heard about the funeral. I would assume it would be soon though." The woman tapped her fingernails against the back of the couch. "So, about this piece of watermelon delight? Whaddaya say? It can be delivered tomorrow."

※※※

Babe at least waited until we were in my car before hurling questions my way. "Well, what did she say? Did you find out anything about Jerry?"

I scowled at Babe. "Maybe you would know if you'd stuck around."

"Do I need to explain to you what the aging process does to

a woman's bladder?"

I closed my eyes. "No, please don't."

"Okay, then, spill it. What did she say?"

"She said she'll have the couch delivered to you by the end of the week."

Babe narrowed her eyes. "Very funny. If you ordered that couch for me, I wouldn't be your friend anymore."

My chin dipped down as I drew in a deep breath, fighting frustration. "You're the one who placed me in that position!"

Babe grinned and I knew she was trying to "get my goat," as she liked to say. No, the expression wasn't teen slang. Apparently, it meant she was trying to annoy me. She claims the saying has French origins, so therefore it was still cool to use it.

"So?"

I shrugged. "I didn't really find out anything."

"Oh, come on. I know you snooped! You had to."

"You're the snooper. Not me." Silence fell as miles of countryside rolled past our windows. I mulled over theories. Finally, I asked, "What do you know about Yvonne?"

"She doesn't live in Boring."

"Yeah, she mentioned that. Plus, I'd figured that since I'd never seen her around." How sad that I'd started to know everyone in town already. Growing up in Cincinnati, I didn't even know everyone in my high school class.

"Jerry handpicked her to work at the store."

I didn't know what to say, but something just didn't sit right with Babe's statement. "That must have been—an honor? To be handpicked to work at that store."

Babe snapped her fingers in a Z pattern. "Fo'sure, chickaroonie." Babe must have been reading an urban dictionary before going to bed at night. "Why would someone drive all the way down here to work at a couch store for more than a decade?"

"There are plenty of furniture stores in Indy that probably pay better, and they're closer to where she lives. It doesn't make sense. Unless—"

"She and Jerry are having an affair! My thoughts exactly."

My shoulders dropped. "I was going to say, 'Unless The Couch King has really good benefits.'" We came to the town's only stoplight and I took the opportunity to stare at Babe, dumbfounded. "How did you connect those dots?"

"The rumor has been circulating around town for a long time." Babe shrugged, as nonchalant as ever.

I held back a sigh. The light turned green and gave my mouth permission to go. "Candace worked at the store. Wouldn't she have known something was going on? I mean, if you're going to have an affair, you should be a little secretive about it, right?"

"I don't know. It sounds like a motive for murder to me."

I added two names to my mental list of who could have killed Candace: Jerry and Yvonne. But no one had seen Jerry for days, and I had serious doubts that Yvonne had been the one to stick a note in my mailbox. Unless she was a great actress, she truly seemed to have no idea who I was. Which left me back at square one.

# 7

Babe and I decided to stop by the pharmacy for lunch. We parked at a metered space out front and walked into the store, which was located on the corner of our cozy little downtown area. The business was more than one-hundred years old and had black and white tiles checkering the floor. At the front were various items from hair care products to toy John Deere tractors. At the back wall was the pharmacy, and at the L beyond that was a little ice cream counter that also sold sandwiches and chips. The place was quaint, I had to give it that.

Kent spotted us from his position in the back, but only had time for a smile and a wave as we walked in. Since a majority of the population in Boring was in their golden years, and this was the only pharmacy in town, Kent kept busy. He had one employee who helped him, a dark-haired girl named Jasmine.

I watched Kent for a moment as he talked to a white-haired woman. I could tell he loved it here. He positively beamed behind that counter.

The store where he'd worked in Chicago had been large; though the benefits were good, the pressure had been overwhelming. At 28 years old, he should have been energetic and enjoying his job. But his skin always looked pale, and he dreaded going to work every morning. Then the "incident" at my work had taken place, followed up by a second "incident" where someone had pulled a knife on me and stolen my purse.

After that, Kent had sat down with me and told me about this wild dream he had to move to a small town and run his own pharmacy. He wanted a slower pace of life, especially if we were going to have kids one day. He'd grown up in a small town and loved it.

I'd looked at him like he was crazy.

But I loved him, so I agreed to explore the options.

That's when he found a pharmacy for sale in Boring, Indiana. He went alone to visit one day—I had to work—and when he came back home, he couldn't stop talking about the place. He thought the town would be the ideal location for a family. The city was no place to have kids, he said. I just had to visit.

So I did.

That night when we got home, after Kent was asleep, I'd cried. And cried. Boring was the last place I wanted to be. But I knew this was where we'd end up because I loved my husband more than I loved the city.

"How'd you meet your husband, Babe?" I asked before taking a bite of my grilled cheese sandwich. Her husband had passed away years ago, but I knew Babe didn't mind talking about him. He'd owned a chain of banks up in Indy. Babe moved down here after he passed away. Apparently, he'd left her very comfortable.

"I worked at one of his banks. I was the beautiful young teller, and he was my rich, handsome boss. It was quite the scandal when we started dating."

"Scandal?" This I wanted to hear.

"He was fifteen years old than me."

Someone had robbed the cradle. Who would have thought? "Was it love at first sight?"

Her eyes got a faraway look that made me envy her. "You might say that. We played games with each other, teasing and flirting. It was such fun."

For some pessimistic reason, I wanted to pop that dreamy look out of her eyes. "And let me guess—you got married and that all went away?"

"Of course not! It got even better."

My heart sunk. "Oh. That's great." And it was. For her. Not me.

"Not many marriages were like ours. We had something special." Babe took a sideways glance at me. "You and Kent do too, honey. Of course."

"I'm not so sure lately."

I glanced over at him and saw him laughing with Jasmine. We used to laugh together.

"How long have you been married?"

"Seven years next week."

She patted my shoulder. "Every marriage has rough patches. The good news is they're just patches. There's a whole bunch of smooth road beyond that."

I smiled. "Thanks, Babe."

As much as Babe drove me crazy, I wanted to tell her about the note. I needed to share the information with someone. Surely I could trust Babe, who might be a hardhead but still trustworthy. I pushed my plate away. "Babe—"

Two women from church rounded the corner and sat at the counter next to us.

Babe looked at me, waiting for me to continue. "Yes?"

I glanced at the ladies from church and shook my head. "Never mind. It's not important."

※※※

Babe and I left a few minutes later. We decided to take a stroll down Main Street to walk off the extra calories we'd consumed. I walked along the storefronts, past the Pronto Café. Just ahead was what town folk's affectionately called "Grandpa's." The real name of the antique store had outgrown the marquee. The owner called it the Jacob, Emily, Martin, Ann, James and Marlyn Shop. Every time a new grandchild was born, he added to the marquee.

Then there was the courthouse and an old cemetery. At the corner stood a grand bank, complete with real marble fixtures and a second story balcony. I paused outside the massive wooden doors.

"I need to take some cash out. Do you mind?" I grasped the thick handle.

Babe swung her head back and forth while pursing her lips. "You won't catch me in that bank."

I raised an eyebrow, counted to three, and finally asked, "Why not? Boring National is the only bank in town."

"That Paul Willis drives me crazy! I'm not going to give his business one single cent."

Paul Willis owned the bank. We went to church together and he always seemed like a nice enough man. I paused, feeling somewhat like a therapist. "What do you have against Mr. Willis?"

"He thinks he's smooth, talking about how he used to hang around with all of the cool cats back in the day." She swung her hand through the air, snapping her fingers in her signature motion. "Or maybe I should say, 'He thinks he's all that and a bag of chips.'" Dramatically, she crossed her arms and scowled. "He's a faker, that's what he is."

I nodded slowly, trying to comprehend. I finally settled on, "I'll just be a moment."

Babe scowled harder. "I'm waiting out here."

"Fine." I gripped my purse, ready to go inside.

"In the cold."

I shrugged, pushing away my guilt. "It's your choice."

Her lips parted—in surprise, I assumed. "You'd leave an old woman in the cold?"

My shoulders slumped in exasperation. "Babe! You're an

adult. You're making your own choices." I had to get a grip on this pushover thing before it became my standard. Today, I'd take my stand.

Babe harrumphed as I pulled the heavy door open. No little bells jingled as I stepped inside the bank. In fact, it seemed awfully quiet, quiet enough that I took a step back to check the hours posted out front. Closed. The bank should be closed.

That was one thing I'd discovered about small town life. Businesses were open at odd hours and never, ever on holidays, even on President's Day or Memorial Day. It seemed like whenever my parents came to visit, everything was always closed. Even the post office kept strange hours, and I could never remember when it was open and when it wasn't.

But if the bank was closed for a lunch break right now, why was the door unlocked?

I stuck my head inside. No tellers stood behind their wood-framed windows. No management greeted me. No customers milled about.

Okay, so there were only three people who worked at the bank, but still, someone should have been out front, or the doors should have been locked.

"Hello?" My voice echoed off the high ceilings.

Even no music whispered from the overhead speakers, I realized. Mr. Willis usually put in a jazz CD for customers to enjoy. Back in the day, he'd played saxophone at a club up in Chicago. We'd talked about it at church before.

I stepped further inside and said hello again.

No answer. The teller windows were to my left, and directly in front of me stood the vault. I glanced at it quickly, relieved to see the door closed. Had the place been robbed and all the tellers locked in the vault? That would explain why no one was around. Or was my imagination working on overtime since Candace died? That was the most likely scenario.

I decided to step closer to the vault, just to make sure there wasn't anyone inside screaming for help. I couldn't call the police every time I had a crazy hunch. Most of the time, I was wrong. I tiptoed across the floor until I reached the massive steel door. Carefully, I propelled my ear until it touched the cool metal.

Silence.

A hallway stretched beyond the vault. I stepped in that direction, and heard a TV blaring. My stomach clenched. Flashbacks of finding Candace assaulted my memory.

"Mr. Willis?"

Still no one appeared. Perhaps he'd stepped out for a bit. But why would he leave his bank unlocked? People in Boring weren't that trusting. And Mr. Willis wasn't that stupid.

I followed the sound of the TV until I reached a room marked "Employees Only." I knocked. I could hear the TV on the other side. Taking a deep breath, I cracked the door open. "Mr. Willis?"

The TV sat on a table against the far wall. The back of a couch faced me. No one in here.

As I was about to close the door, I froze and closed my eyes. That wasn't what I thought.

It wasn't.

Couldn't be.

I forced my eyes open and stepped forward, squinting.

Yes, that did appear to be a leather shoe resting on the arm of the couch. The position of the shoe made it clear that the footwear was attached to a leg.

Lord, be with me. I paused and looked at the ceiling. Then at whomever that foot belonged to.

I took another step and peered over the back of the couch. That's when I saw Mr. Willis—lying on the couch like a corpse.

# 8

I screamed.

All of a sudden, Mr. Willis rose from the dead.

He darted from the couch, looking as if I'd scared him to death—or scared him to life, however you wanted to look at it.

"What are you doing?" he shouted, clutching his chest. "What's going on? How'd you get in here?"

"You're alive!"

"Of course I'm alive, girl. I'm old, not dead."

Babe burst through the door. Her eyes were wide and her pink lipstick freshly applied. "What happened? Are you okay? What did I miss?"

I pressed a hand over my heart, which pounded erratically in my ears. Finally, I laughed a shaky laugh and pointed at Mr. Willis. "I thought you were dead."

I could see the headlines now: Attack of the Killer Couches.

"Dead? Not yet. Keep sneaking up on me like that and I might be soon." Mr. Willis grabbed a fedora from the hat rack and slipped it over his balding head. His gaze flickered behind me to Babe. "And how are you doing today, Ms. Pritchard?"

She stuck her nose in the air. "Just fine, no thanks to you."

"To me? What did I do? I was just back here taking a nap. It was the two of you who barged in!" His gaze swung back and forth between us.

Babe harrumphed. "I came in only because I heard my friend scream. I had no intention of entering your establishment."

He stepped closer. "Afraid you might find something you like?"

Babe crossed her arms and leaned forward, an unusual firmness in her inflection. "Not a chance."

The tension in the room was tight enough to make me snap. "I'm glad you're okay, Mr. Willis. I was only concerned for your well-being. Babe, I'll come back another time—when you're not with me. I can see this was a bad idea."

The two still faced off. I watched them to see who would blink first. Instead, they stared, Babe with fire in her eyes and Mr. Willis with a twinkle.

"There are plenty of other banks around," Babe said.

"But this one is the best."

"Says who?"

"Says me." Mr. Willis looked rather smug.

I grabbed Babe's arm before war broke out. "Come on, let's go." I pulled her away. "I'm glad you're okay, Mr. Willis!

You should really make sure those front doors are locked when you're closed."

"Sorry about that scare, and I will talk to the manager about those doors being left unlocked. It's unacceptable. Plain unacceptable!"

As soon as we were out of earshot, I whispered, "What was that about?"

"He rubs me the wrong way."

I looked at Babe. "Because he thinks he's a 'cool cat'?"

She shrugged like an adolescent. "Maybe."

"That's ridiculous."

"I don't think so."

There was obviously something going on here that I wasn't picking up on. I'd find out more of the story later. Right now, I needed to get Babe home. We had a big night coming up: our first shift as official Neighborhood Watch volunteers.

✻✻✻

"It's very important as a member of the Neighborhood Watch Patrol that you're always on alert." Harry cruised through our neighborhood in his beat-up Seville. Darkness had fallen several hours ago, and no one stirred—except us. "The bad guys are sneaky—very sneaky. You have to keep your ears open and your eyes peeled."

I rolled my eyes in the backseat and shoved some copies of Body Building magazine onto the floor. They collided with a hodgepodge of empty protein shake containers and a few apple cores. And this guy wondered why he couldn't get a date? I hoped he never asked me my opinion on the matter because I would be forced to confront him with the truth. He was a slob, self-obsessed, and he had bad breath. There.

Babe sat up front as Harry "trained" us for this new position. Did this guy always take himself so seriously?

"I'm jiggy with it." Babe angled her hands in front of her like a rapper.

And did Babe ever take herself seriously? Only when she was around Paul Willis, apparently.

"If you see anyone sneaking around, you'll want to report it to the police. That includes anyone dodging behind cars, bushes, or in people's backyards. You can never be too careful, especially in light of recent events."

Yeah, Candace. Poor thing. Was there any hope of anyone solving her murder?

As Harry rambled on and on about how important it was for us to keep our neighborhood safe, I thought about Kent.

I'd only seen him for five minutes when he got home from work. He was late—again. The chicken pot pie I had prepared for him—made only with ingredients that were sealed and I was sure hadn't been tampered with—was cold when he'd arrived home. He didn't seem bothered by it, but I was.

And I'd wanted to tell him about my day, about Babe and The Couch King.

Before I could get in a word, he'd blurted, "I think I need a man cave."

I'd stopped in my tracks. "A what?"

"A man cave. You know, a place of my own where I can do my own thing." In other words, a place where he could spend his time without me.

"And why do you think you need this?"

He shrugged. "I don't know. It just seems like the suburban thing to do. I'm thinking I could turn the garage into my space. You know, put in an old TV and couch. Maybe a small refrigerator. Hang up some sports paraphernalia and a few strands of string lights. Then I can invite the guys from church over to watch the game sometime."

At that moment, I felt more and more of our marriage slipping away.

As I left, he'd taken his nuked dinner and plopped in front of the TV to watch *Judge Judy*. Part of me wondered if he was glad I'd left so he could spend uninterrupted time with Panny, my loving nickname for our Panasonic.

"Do you have any questions, Laura?"

"What?" My gaze refocused on Harry, who tried to preen in the rearview mirror while catching a glimpse of me.

He shined his front teeth with his finger then flickered his gaze back to me. "Do you understand what your responsibilities are?"

"Of course."

"Tomorrow night will be your shift. I figure you can have Tuesdays and Thursdays. I'll take the rest of the week."

"Sure."

"I feel like I'm on the TV show *Cops*! This is so exciting." Babe clapped her hands before abruptly pointing in the distance. "Did I just see movement over there?"

Harry grinned. "Let's go check it out."

I rolled my eyes again. I'd seen movement too. It wasn't a cat burglar. It was just a plain cat.

Harry spotlighted the feline with his headlights and shook his head, as if disappointed.

This would be a good time to chat about Candace, I figured. I leaned forward, in between the seats. "So Harry, do you have any theories as to what happened to Candace? You're 'in the know' with things around here. Certainly, you have some ideas."

He puffed his chest out. "Of course I have ideas. They're just speculation right now, though. I have to prove I'm right."

Then maybe Romeo would allow him to be a part of the police department, I thought. Poor guy wanted something he could likely never have. I understood all about that. My big city dreams had been dashed when I moved here.

I leaned farther between the seats. "Come on. Just share with us. We're a team now. Maybe we can even help you."

Babe glanced back at me, admiration in her eyes.

"Well, I do have one main suspect who stands out in my mind."

I leaned closer. "Who?"

"This is just between the three of us. I don't want any rumors being spread around." He glanced back at us, like a father giving his children a warning.

I rolled my eyes when I was sure he couldn't see me. "Of course."

"Okay, you both seem pretty trustworthy. And maybe you should know this information since you're both a part of Neighborhood Watch. You never can be too careful." He pulled to a stop at the side of the road and cut off his headlights before shifting in his seat to face us. "Donna."

"Donna?" Why on earth would he think Donna was guilty? Donna was Mrs. Prim and Proper. Of course, Tiara had acted like something was stressing her friend out. Could something have been stressing her out enough to murder someone?

"I saw Candace and Donna arguing last week."

"Arguing about what?"

Harry shrugged. "I wasn't close enough to hear, but it looked pretty heated."

"Well, spit it out. What's your theory?" Babe didn't mince words.

Harry drew in a deep breath, as if he were hesitant to share. Something about the action didn't ring quite true to me, though. "You know Donna is opposing Hillary in the next election? She wants to be president of the Homeowners' Association."

"She does?" It was the first I'd heard of it. If I understood correctly, no one had ever dared to run against Hillary. Besides that, I'd never seen Donna as the type to have an interest in politics at any level. She seemed content being a family woman. And her kids sure kept her busy between all of their activities.

"It's the only thing I can think of that they would have been arguing about."

"But why would Candace and Donna be arguing over that?" I raised my palm in the air in confusion. "Candace and Donna were friends. Certainly Candace would have supported her in the election process. Everyone knows Candace didn't like Hillary."

Harry brushed his mustache with his fingers. "That's the question I'd like an answer to also."

※※※

My investigation was not working so far. And it was because I had no plan.

The next morning, as soon as Kent left for work, I sat down with a cup of coffee at my kitchen table and pulled out a notebook. I needed to approach this like a public relations campaign.

Every good public relations campaign had several elements to it. First, I needed an objective. I had that. To find Candace's killer before Candace's killer found me.

Each campaign also required connection and credibility. Connecting meant I needed to get out of this house and interact with people. Draw on all my friendliness and charm. Find out information. Credibility meant I needed to establish trust and inspire confidence.

I could do it. I wouldn't let someone keep me in my own house, scared to come out, scared to eat.

Ever since my attack in Chicago, I'd vowed never, ever to let someone make me feel weak again. Even though fear still simmered beneath my bravado, I was determined to push through it. That's what made people strong.

Being a city slicker just might come in handy now, I realized.

My first goal today would be to introduce myself to my new neighbors who'd moved in two doors down. After all, that's what people in the 'burbs did.

The sun shone brightly as I charged up the sidewalk and rapped on the front door. I should have brought something with me, a plate of cookies or brownies. Donna would have done that.

A woman with brown hair, so dark it was almost black, clacked toward the storm door in high heels, a top with a plunging neckline, tight black pants, and way too much jewelry. "Yes?"

"I just thought I'd introduce myself. I'm Laura Berry, and I live two houses down from you."

A smile grazed her lips but didn't reach her eyes. "Hi, I'm Gia." She held out a manicured hand, tipped with blood-red fingernail polish.

I reached for it and attempted a handshake, but her grip felt so limp that it gave me the shivers. I pulled back and rubbed my hand on my jeans. Awkward silence chirped between us.

I cleared my throat. Charming. Persuasive. Credible. Get with it, Laura! "So, today's the big day, huh? Moving's no fun. I just moved here myself nine months ago. Finally I won't be the new kid on the block."

A man paced into the room behind her, a phone glued to his ear. From where I stood, he looked like Marlon Brando from *The Godfather* days. He stopped at the base of the stairs and grunted. "I'm going to make him an offer he can't refuse."

What did that mean? An offer who couldn't refuse? Was it just me or were there threatening undertones to that statement?

He snapped his cell phone shut and walked toward us. A warm smile spread over his face. "And who do we have here?"

"Our new neighbor, Lori."

"Laura."

The man raised his head slowly, his gaze never leaving me. "Good to meet you, Lauren. I'm Steele. We look forward to getting to know you."

New York accent. Definitely a New York accent. The rumor around town had been that they were from Virginia.

"Long trip here today?" I asked Gia.

She shrugged, looking at a chip on her nails. She had the detachment of someone who'd lived in the city. Could this woman be my new best friend?

There was a small problem. I realized, right then, that I didn't miss the detachedness of urban dwellers. "I got here a few days ago," she said. "Steele just got here today."

A few days ago. That meant she arrived just in time for—

"I saw the police down the street the other day. There something I should know about this neighborhood?" Gia's thin eyebrows arched together, and she turned her attention from her fingertips.

"It's usually pretty dull."

"Then what happened at that house?" She pointed at the Flynns'. Suddenly, I had her full attention.

I tried to think of a way to word it nicely, without the murder sounding so evil. How could I say it with cushion, though? Murder was murder. There was nothing nice about it.

"I met the man who lives there. What was his name?" Gia tapped her pointy-toe shoe against the tiled entryway. "Larry? Gary?"

My insides went ice cold. "Jerry?"

She snapped her fingers, a near miracle for someone with nails her length. "That's it. I met Jerry. He seems like a nice enough man."

"When did you say you got here?"

"Five or six days ago."

Five or six days ago. When Jerry was supposed to be out of town.

# 9

My phone chirped when I stepped back into my house. Icicles were already running through my veins after Gia's announcement. And that video of me had been filmed from inside Jerry's house. He was quickly moving up on my list of suspects.

Psycho, stupid, tech savvy. Check, check, and, based on all of the commercials he'd been in, Jerry had to have some kind of knowledge of cameras, right? So, check.

I needed to talk to Kent. Needed to tell him what was going on. Who else could I trust? Babe? I loved her, but she had a tendency to blab things all over town.

I slammed the front door shut behind me, warding away the cold. It didn't work. My phone chirped again, so I reached into my back pocket. I didn't recognize the number, but I put it to my ear and answered anyway.

Static crackled on the other line. "Hello?"

Finally, a tinny, masculine voice came through the line. "How about we get away for the weekend? Maybe that will help you forget."

"Really?" a woman said in the background. "You can get away from your job for that long?"

I straightened, my pulse suddenly pounding. Why did the voice sound familiar? The conversation seem like a rerun? Had someone butt dialed me?

"Let me think this through. I can't do it this weekend," the man said. "I don't have anyone to fill in for me."

"Can't people take their prescriptions up to Indy just for this weekend?"

I sucked in a breath. This was a real conversation. A conversation Kent and I had just a couple of days ago right here in my living room. Despite my horror, I couldn't stop listening.

"I'm trying to establish people's trust, Laura. You know how skeptical the locals feel about outsiders. People thought when I bought their local pharmacy that I'd never succeed with my big city values. I have to prove to them that I'm trustworthy and dependable. How about next weekend instead?"

"That's the bake sale at church that I promised to help out with."

"There's always the weekend after that. We have the rest of our lives, sweetheart."

"Of course."

"Honey—"

"Really, it's okay. I told you I would support you in this new chapter of our lives, and I am. I just didn't say I would have fun while doing so."

"I couldn't ask for a better wife."

I wasn't sure what was stronger—my fear over hearing this conversation, or my despair over my marriage.

Another voice came on the line, this one modulated by electronics. "See, I told you I was listening, Laura Berry. I have eyes and ears everywhere. Spill any beans and you die. Same goes for your husband."

The line went dead.

The phone dropped from my hand and hit the floor, scattering into pieces. How had someone taped that conversation? There had to be a bug in this house.

Cold chills raced up my spine. I'd thought I was being paranoid. But I wasn't being paranoid at all.

Knocking sounded in my backyard again.

Babe. Trying to get something out of the shed. I was not in the mood for this right now. Didn't I just tell her that there was a killer on the loose and that she had to be more careful?

I stormed toward the back door, ready to remind her—in a loving, respectful way, of course.

As soon as I reached the door, a huge ball of flames rocketed toward the sky.

My shed was on fire.

# 10

Three hours later, fire and police personnel had cleared off my property after the flames had been extinguished. The source of the fire had been an old propane tank. Chief Romeo seemed to believe the blaze was accidental, but I had other theories.

I'd called Kent earlier as the fire crew was on the scene, and he'd asked if I needed him at home. I said no, though part of me wanted to scream, "Yes! Yes, of course I need you at home!"

At the moment, I stood in the middle of my living room, the silence frightening.

How had someone recorded my conversation with Kent?

My gaze roamed over the couch, the stylish recliners, and the end tables. There was a bug somewhere in the house. I had to find it. Now.

I could have told Chief Romeo about it, only the person who planted the device might have heard me and done something else terrible and awful to my family. He—or she—might have decided to start with blowing up our shed and then move on to blowing up our house.

I tiptoed to my computer, berating myself for sneaking around my own house. That's how it felt when your privacy had been invaded, though. I was an outsider in my own home.

After sitting down at the computer, I quickly did an Internet search for "how to find listening devices." Pages of results popped up.

Information assimilated, I rummaged around in my laundry room until I found an old radio. Then I flipped the switch to "on" and walked into my living room, to the area where Kent and I'd had our conversation.

The articles I'd read said my radio would start to squeal when it got close to the bug. The Bangles sang "Walk Like an Egyptian" as I skulked around my house, occasionally feeling the need to break out into the sand dance.

The radio remained the same around my couch, my chairs, the breakfast bar. Where would someone plant a listening device? I'd seen pictures of a few online, and I knew they were so small they could fit nearly anywhere.

As I passed an end table, the radio squealed. I paused and stepped closer. The squeals and static became louder.

I set the radio on the ground. My throat went dry as I picked up a picture of me and Kent. I turned it over and searched the back of the frame. My fingers brushed something underneath the stand, neatly camouflaged by the black cardboard leg that propped it up.

I held up the small plastic device, no bigger than a quarter.

Who in the world in Boring had access to technology like this? Who'd been able to sneak into my home and plant it when I wasn't around? What kind of person had set up shop in the Flynns' house so they could videotape me?

Chills raced across my skin.

I had no idea.

But I was going to find out.

※※※

When I stepped into the Pronto Café thirty minutes later, all of the chatter zapped into silence. People stared at me, their food frozen halfway into their mouths.

I knew what they were saying before I'd interrupted their gossip.

That city slicker. Left the tank for her gas grill open and when the light bulb in the shed mysteriously sparked, the whole place went up in the flames.

If I was to voice my concern that someone had purposefully set my shed on fire, I'd only sound paranoid. Instead, I ignored everyone—but only because I wanted to keep my "connection and credibility" legit—and I stomped over to the corner booth where I could listen to life take place all around me. I hadn't ordered their specialty, green eggs and ham. No, I was in the mood for a half-pound burger, loaded with bacon, cheese and mayo. Oh, and I wanted fries with plenty of salt on them. I wouldn't dip them in ketchup—that condiment seemed too much like a vegetable. I wanted ranch dressing. Just for kicks, I ordered a full-strength, highly-caffeinated, liquid-sugar soda.

After I'd found the bugging device, I'd dropped it down the garbage disposal, my stomach tight with anxiety as I'd listened to the plastic crack and shred as my sink digested it. At that point, I'd given up any thoughts of cooking dinner and come here to the café.

It didn't matter. It wasn't like Kent would make it home in time to eat together. No doubt this would be another long day at the pharmacy, as well as another long day of me feeling disconnected and utterly alone, not to exaggerate or anything. I mean, what kind of husband didn't come home when something on his property was ablaze? I knew Kent thought I was self-sufficient, but really? *Really?*

Did he not know that someone had bugged our home? That someone had sent me a threatening note? Okay. I guess he didn't know. But still—shouldn't he be able to read my mind?

I savored each bite of my meal as I watched the TV perched high in the corner. Dr. Phil giving marriage advice. Maybe I'd learn something.

I never thought I'd be one to need marriage advice. Never. Kent and I both came from stable homes. We had good educations and had dated a respectable two years before marrying. What did we have to worry about? Obviously, I should have listened more in our premarriage counseling courses. Certainly you weren't supposed to feel so disconnected in a good marriage.

I tuned Dr. Phil out. Thinking about my marriage was getting me nowhere except deeper into my tense ball of stress.

Beside me, Emma Jean chatted—rather loudly, I might add—with the owner of Pronto, Barbara Ann, about the way the town used to be. Two golfers sat on the other side of me, and they might as well have been speaking a different language. Two men three seats over talked about the upcoming Ginseng Festival here in Boring.

My ears perked when someone in a booth behind me mentioned Candace. I took a sip of my soda and leaned back, trying to eavesdrop. Yes, my mother taught me manners. I just chose to forget them for the time being.

A female voice said, "Everyone knows that Jerry's a no-good cheater."

"But that doesn't make him a killer."

"Who do you think did it, then?"

"Maybe it was—"

"Fancy seeing you here, chickaroonie!"

I jumped and splashed soda all over my blouse. I gasped and grabbed a napkin as the icy liquid chilled my skin. "Babe!"

"Thought you saw me come in. Sorry 'bout that." She slid onto the seat across from me and ordered some hot chocolate. "Cold day out there."

"Even colder now," I muttered, still wiping at my wet shirt. She didn't seem to hear me or notice the spill. Maybe it was the sunglasses she was wearing—stylishly oversized and so dark I'm surprised she recognized me.

"Heard about your shed. Freaky."

"Freaky," I repeated. And it was. How much could I tell Babe? Could I tell her about the threats? The phone call? The letter? No, I decided. The fewer people who knew, the better.

Babe reapplied her pink lipstick under the guidance of the mirror on her powder compress. "Shouldn't you be at home cooking for Kent?"

I scowled, and threw my napkin on the counter. "He's working late."

She lowered the mirror and peered at me. "Doing that a lot lately, huh?"

"Yeah."

"Could be worse. He could be lazy like Jerry."

I nodded. "Point taken." I ignored the chilly liquid splattered across the front of my shirt and turned toward my friend. "Babe, I just met my new neighbors—"

"Are they nice? Italian, I hear. I bet she makes a mean meatball."

"Yes, but that's beside the point. The woman—Gia is her name—she said that she saw Jerry after she arrived in Boring. She moved here four or five days ago—when Jerry was supposed to be out of town."

"Now that's juicy news."

"Should I go to the police with it?"

"Probably. They'll figure things out. I hope."

I raised an eyebrow. I hope. My thoughts exactly. Just how reliable were the police here in Boring, Indiana? I'd bet they spent more time playing Halo than they did solving real crimes.

They had the bellies to prove it.

Babe eyed my meal.

"I always took you as more of a salad type of girl," Babe said.

"I'm splurging." So were my hips, but no need to mention that.

I glanced over my shoulder quickly, trying to get a glimpse of who had been mentioning Jerry a moment ago. Of course, who in town hadn't been mentioning Jerry lately? I spotted a lady from church and her sister sipping milkshakes. I couldn't remember their names, but they seemed nice enough. Their voices were low now, and I couldn't make out a thing they said.

"Everything okay?" Babe snitched one of my fries.

I shrugged. "I suppose. After I eat this heart attack on a plate, I guess I'll make my way over to the police station. I'll see what they say about Jerry. Maybe they have an update."

※※※

"Take that, scum bag!"

Okay, so it wasn't the combat video game Halo. It was video game Mortal Combat. But there Chief Romeo and Officer Maloney were, sitting in a back office at the police station with controllers in their hands. They didn't even hear me come in.

I cleared my throat and set my purse on the front desk with a loud thump. Both men jumped, dropping their remotes, and tripped over themselves to get to the front. Officer Maloney's face flushed. I had to give him credit for at least looking embarrassed. I supposed if they couldn't catch the real bad guys, maybe it made them feel better to catch fake, video game ones.

"Well, hello Mrs. Berry. What brings you in?" Romeo tucked his shirt into his pants as he approached me at the desk. Beyond him I could see an empty jail cell—a jail cell where a killer should be right now. Candace may not have been well liked, but she deserved justice. Everyone did.

I glanced at the TV screen as it flicked to black. "How's the investigation going? I'm surprised you're not still at my house after the shed exploded."

Chief Romeo laughed, but it sounded fake, especially when his chuckles died in a fit of coughing. "Now, aren't you a concerned citizen? Despite what people around here say about you city slickers, you really do care, don't you?" He cleared his throat again. "I've done everything I can pertaining to your shed. Now it's the fire chief's job."

I stared at him, pondering my reaction. Finally, I nodded and said, "So, about the investigation into Candace's death?"

His smile disappeared. "We're following up on every lead. Have some strong suspects."

I glanced at the blank TV screen. "I can see."

He finished tucking his shirt in, and I noticed sweat beads appear on his forehead. "What can I help you with?"

I shared my discovery. Romeo nodded and jotted down notes on his desk calendar. The cops in Chicago would have never stood for this. When I'd been attacked, it had taken them less than 24 hours to track down the man who'd held a knife to my throat in the alleyway beside my apartment building.

Don't get me wrong—I don't think all small-town police departments are inept. Just this one. I'd do a better job than they did. And I just might end up proving that fact.

"We'll look into it, ma'am."

I stared at Romeo for a moment, trying to find some measure of confidence. Nothing. I couldn't even fake a look of trust. Should I tell him about the phone call? The threatening note? No, I decided. It wouldn't do any good.

I nodded. "I'll be going then."

I climbed back into my 4Runner and locked the doors—a killer was on the loose, after all. It could be anyone in this sleepy little town. I soaked in Boring in all of its glory as I drove back home. The town had its charm, that's for sure. Main Street was lit with lanterns and the sidewalks were cobblestone. Little benches were placed every so often to add to the ambiance. Just past downtown was the General Store, and across the street from that the high school, where we had our Homeowners' Association meetings. Old houses, original to the town, scattered behind those buildings on neat little streets.

Beyond those houses were fields of ginseng. I'm not sure how Boring ended up being a major producer of ginseng, but it had. Ironically, ginseng helped people stay awake. How appropriate.

Apparently, they had a big festival every year where they served everything from ginseng tea to ginseng ice cream. Now that I thought about it, that festival should be coming up soon.

I'd heard the buzz about it going around town, and there had even been a couple of articles in the paper.

The next turn was into our neighborhood—the worst thing that could happen to Boring, according to many. Suburbia had come to Boring, and Boring didn't particularly welcome the new faces. But Hillary's husband, a developer, had purchased the land and built the homes about a decade ago. Slowly, they were filling up. Many people from Indianapolis moved down here to get away from the crime of the city.

A few of the town's "originals" had eventually moved into the neighborhood. Those houses were bigger and closer to the golf course, which had also gone up with the neighborhood. No one complained about that.

As I drove into my cul-de-sac, I noticed everything seemed especially dark. I pulled into the driveway and saw that my house had no lights on.

I glanced at my watch. Eight o'clock. What was Kent doing at this hour that required the whole house to be black? Had he gone to sleep already? His car was in the driveway, so he was home.

A terrible thought entered my mind. What if the killer had knocked Kent off also? What if some of those sleeping pills had gotten onto his food? I should have warned him to watch what he ate! I should have monitored his sack lunches better, maybe even insisted that he grab a bite at the pharmacy.

I jumped out of my car and ran to my front door. My fingers fumbled until finally the key pushed into the lock. I twisted and the door opened.

My heart beat in my throat as I stepped inside. Thankfully, I didn't hear a TV in the background.

"Kent? Kent? Are you home?"

I flicked the lights in the foyer. My house remained black. What was going on?

I slowly crept forward. My hand stretched in front of me, feeling for any obstacles. Hand me a lantern, and I could make the cover of an old Nancy Drew novel. I felt like I was in a scene right out of one of her old books. Only my house wasn't nearly creepy enough.

Kent's car was in the driveway, so I knew he'd been here. Maybe he'd simply gone to visit one of the neighbors. Still, something felt wrong.

*Please, Lord, let Kent be okay.*

I pictured Candace, and nausea churned in my gut. I might've been upset with my husband, but I wasn't ready to let him go yet. This couldn't be the end.

"Kent?" I called again, my voice shaky this time.

I rounded the corner into the living room, my hand brushing the wall to keep me steady. I could only make out the outline of my furniture—the couch, the TV, and a couple of end tables. No Kent. Where could he be? I'd check the bedrooms before calling the police.

I turned around to go upstairs when I collided with someone. A killer?

I screamed and my hands flew into the air, along with my

leftovers.

Kent pulled the headphones from his ear. "Laura? What's the matter with you? Where have you been?"

"Kent!" I threw myself into his arms, drinking in the scent of his aftershave. I could still hear the strands from a Casting Crowns' song drifting from his MP3 player and through his earphones. "You're okay. You're okay. I was so worried."

He patted my back as if I were a small, naive child. "Of course I'm okay. What did you think? I ate poisoned pork rinds?"

I backed out of his embrace and scowled. He had no idea. My feelings must have shown through to my face because his goofy grin disappeared and he brushed my cheek with his fingers.

"Oh Laura, I'm sorry." He pulled me into his chest. "I shouldn't have said that. I'm sure you're still going through post traumatic stress and—"

I backed out of his arms. "Post traumatic stress? Is that what you call it? How about calling it what it is? I saw my friend dead." My voice grew louder with each word and my hands pounded each other to emphasize my point.

His eyes softened. "You're right. I'm sorry, Laura. Can we start over?"

I hung my head for a moment. I had to get a grip. What was wrong with me? Flying off the handle wasn't like me. "Yes, of course we can."

He took my elbow. "Let's go sit down. I'll fix you a cup of tea, and we can talk."

I plopped on the couch while he wandered into the kitchen.

I heard the clanging of the metal teapot as Kent set it on the burner. I heard the clanking of my teacups as he pulled one from the cabinet. While he waited for the water to boil, he came and sat beside me.

I glanced over at him. "Why are the lights off?"

"I guess our entire cul-de-sac is without power. I have no idea why."

Fortunately we had a gas stove and a match.

"Where have you been?" Kent pushed his glasses up on his nose. The edge of my lip started to curl. I used to love it when he did that.

"I grabbed a bite to eat. I didn't know when you'd be home."

"I know. I'm so sorry about that. I had too many prescriptions to fill. When people need medicine, they can't wait. Their health depends on my timeliness. Getting the business off the ground is a lot of work."

"But you're glad you did it, right?" Please don't say we've gone through all of these life changes for no good reason.

He grinned. "Absolutely."

The teapot screamed and Kent retreated into the kitchen. A moment later, he reappeared with two steaming drinks. He set them on the coffee table.

"Did you have dinner yet?" I asked, guilt suddenly pounding at my temples.

"No, I just got home."

I reached down to the floor and grabbed the measly doggie bag I'd brought home. It had landed by the couch when Kent surprised me. I offered my husband a half-frown. "I have leftovers."

"That's generous of you, but no thanks." I saw the twinkle in his eyes. "I'll make a sandwich. But first, tell me about the shed. When you said it 'exploded,' you really meant it, didn't you? I had no idea it was that bad."

I nodded. "Yeah, they said something about the propane tanks. I'm still not sure how everything happened."

"The important thing is that you're safe. There have been some strange things happening around here lately. I guess we all need to keep our eyes open."

That sounded like Kent. My Kent.

I would show him how much I supported him, I decided.

Tomorrow, I would buy a couch for his man cave. I would surprise him with a place where he could relax after a hard day's work. He wanted a space of his own, so a space of his own was exactly what I'd give him.

But before I made too many plans to transform our garage into a space that would make ESPN proud, I had to partake in my civic duties.

Tonight was my first night of Neighborhood Watch patrol.

※※※

"I'm driving," I insisted to Babe. The Neighborhood Watch patch on my new shirt irritated my skin underneath. Harry had insisted we had to wear them when on duty. I couldn't be sure, but I'd bet Harry was sitting at his window, counting the number of times he saw us drive by just to make sure we did a good job. He was having trouble releasing his grip as sole citizen patrolman for the neighborhood.

As Babe and I circled the neighborhood, I listened to Babe tell her stories about a Backstreet Boy concert she went to years ago. She even sang a few songs for me, trying to demonstrate how good they sounded. Nothing like her, in other words.

I pulled into our cul-de-sac for the fifth time. Being a part of Neighborhood Watch patrol wasn't nearly as exciting as I'd envisioned. Everyone in the neighborhood appeared to be asleep, except Harry, who at thirty minutes past midnight had found every excuse to be outside, from cleaning his car to searching for a key he dropped on the front lawn.

Finally, I pulled up the car to the curb and rolled down my window. A chilly wind swept inside, instantly cancelling out any heat blowing through the vents. Harry knelt on the ground beside his Seville. "How's it going, Harry? Did you ever find that key?"

He stood and approached the car. He panted and, even in the dark, I could see the dirt patches on his clothing.

"I've been looking. Wish the lights would come back on."

"What happened? The whole neighborhood is out."

"Some idiot must have been doing something stupid." He shrugged. "And now I can't find my house key."

I pointed behind him. "But your front door is open."

"There's a killer out there. I can't have him finding my key."

I nodded. "Good point." Babe nudged me, a signal she wanted to go. "Good luck, Harry. Maybe we'll see you later."

"Seen anything going on tonight?" he asked.

"Absolutely nothing. But if something happens, we'll be sure to report it to you."

We pulled away and continued to cover our "beat."

"Are you always such a kiss-up, chickaroonie?"

I gave Babe a sharp glance. "I'm not a kiss-up, and I resent that comment."

"Resent or resemble?"

Light suddenly appeared in our car—blue and red lights, to be exact. I glanced in the rearview mirror and saw a police cruiser behind us. I pulled over and rolled down my window as Chief Romeo approached, compulsively tucking his shirt in, as always. He leaned on my window, shaking his head when he spotted Babe and me.

"We've had a report of a suspicious car circling the neighborhood."

I pointed to my Neighborhood Watch emblem. "We're on duty. It's our job to circle the neighborhood."

Romeo looked at Babe and me and shook his head. "Harry mentioned you two had volunteered to help out with citizen patrol."

"We just want to keep our cribs safe," Babe called over my shoulder.

I nodded and widened my eyes to look innocent. "Safe."

The chief studied us another moment before standing tall. "Seen anything suspicious going on?"

"All the power's out. Any idea why?" I asked.

"Power company is trying to figure it out now. Hopefully, the electricity will be restored by morning."

I smiled. "Excellent."

The chief took a step away. "Stay out of trouble, you two."

Babe and I giggled as he walked out of earshot.

We began cruising again and Babe propped her feet up on my dashboard. "Like my new kicks?"

Black Converse All-Stars with skulls on them.

"They're—the bomb," I said.

"The bomb!" Babe laughed, as if I sounded ridiculous using that expression.

She had no idea.

As I pulled away from the curb, I figured this might be a good time to approach the subject of Paul Willis. Their encounter had stayed on my mind. "So, how long have you and Mr. Willis known each other?"

Babe scowled and dropped her feet back to the floor before tugging at her stocking cap, which made her look a bit like a burglar. "Long enough."

I'd hit on a touchy subject. I should back off, but I didn't want to. "So you've known him since before you moved to Boring?"

She shrugged and looked out the window. I couldn't be sure, but she might have been pouting. "We ran in the same circles back in my younger days."

There was more to the story! I tapped my fingers on the steering wheel in excitement. "And what circles would that be?"

She remained quiet a moment with her chin in the air. "My

husband and I used to frequent his jazz club."

I tapped my fingers on the steering wheel. "Really? What was it like?"

She shrugged. "It was okay. Nothing special. Every once in awhile he'd bring in some good musicians."

"Isn't that interesting?"

She snorted. "Nothing interesting about it. Now, let's talk about something else."

I glanced at my friend's profile. "I'm just trying to understand why you dislike him so much."

"Some things are just none of your business, Laura."

Babe had a tendency to go from no-holds-barred life of the party to self-righteous prude. Instead of arguing or pointing out her inconsistencies, I continued driving. I looped the whole neighborhood and came back to my street again. I glanced at my house, which looked like every other house in the neighborhood. The builder had only three different styles to choose from, and each one had been a slight variation of the other ones. For as much as we paid for these brick-fronted, vinyl-sided homes, you'd think they'd taken time in putting them up. But no, even on mild days you could feel a breeze coming through the windows and doors. According to Babe, the houses had gone up in three months.

I circled at the end of the street and slowed from 15 to 5 mph as we passed the Flynns'. The house looked even worst in the past week. Sprouts of grass were taller, the weeds seemed to have spread in the flower beds, and the place just looked unloved. Maybe I'd ask Kent to cut the grass sometime.

Movement caught my eye. I gasped and grabbed Babe's arm.

"Something just moved inside the Flynns' house. Look at the curtain!"

Babe leaned forward. "Well, I'll be darned." She slapped her knee and grinned. "Our first excitement of the night. We'd better check it out."

I squeezed her arm as she reached for the door handle. "Oh no, you don't. It's the middle of the night. We should call the police."

"Nonsense. It could be anything. The heat coming on, a fan—"

"A killer." This time, she wasn't talking me into going into the Flynns' house. No way, no chance, no how.

I pulled out my cell phone and the town dispatcher answered. I explained what I'd seen, feeling slightly more official since I got to preface everything with my role on Neighborhood Watch. The dispatcher promised to send out Chief Romeo. In the meantime, Babe and I parked the car outside the house—with the doors locked—just in case someone tried to escape.

# 11

"Nothing to worry about. Just a cat burglar." Chief Romeo held up an orange and white tabby into the nighttime air. "Literally."

"I didn't know they had a cat," I mumbled. I hadn't seen one the day I'd found Candace, nor had I heard her mention one in all of our conversations. That just seemed like a fact I should know. I pulled my arms closer around me, warding off the early morning chill, which, when compounded with the already cold winter air, created one frigid day.

"Hillary made them keep it inside," Babe mumbled, rubbing the cat behind the ears. "She said cats wandering the neighborhood were against the association rules."

Sounded like Hillary. I guess if dogs weren't allowed that freedom, felines shouldn't be either.

Romeo rubbed the beast's head. "This boy looks like he could use a good meal. And a bath. I guess we'll take him down to the animal control shelter."

"No! You can't do that." Babe grabbed Chief Romeo's arm, concern flashing in her sparkling eyes. "That cat needs a home."

"Would you like to take him?" Romeo held out the cat to her.

She waved her hands and took a step back, horror written all over her face. He might as well have asked her to marry him. "Not me. I'm allergic."

In a split second, I felt her gaze on me.

Her index finger shot out, aimed directly at me. "Laura could use a cat."

I, in turn, pointed at myself. In shock, not in agreement. "What? I don't want a cat. I'm a dog lover. Not that I have a dog. Or have ever had a dog. But still. No cats."

Babe nodded, like an over-eager toddler. "Pets make people happy."

"I'm already happy."

She patted my back with a three quick slaps. "Sure you are."

I scowled at Babe. What did she know?

Romeo walked toward his car, the cat protesting in his arms as he did so. "Hopefully, they'll find a home for him at the shelter."

My heart lurched, and I stared at the fuzzy little kitty, whose gaze seemed to be right on me. "And if they don't?" Don't be a pushover, Laura. Develop your backbone.

"Then they have to do the only humane thing."

My eyes widened. "You mean—?"

Romeo nodded.

I gasped. "They can't do that!"

He held the cat out to me. "There's a simple solution."

I snatched the fur ball from his hands. "Fine, but only until you find a home for it." I glanced at the feline. "A home for him." I protectively held the cat to my chest. His sharp nails pulsated through my coat and my neighborhood watch golf shirt into my skin. "Ouch!"

Romeo raised an eyebrow before turning to walk away. "You might want to think about having him de-clawed."

You think? I kept my mouth shut.

As soon as he climbed into his cruiser, I glanced at my watch. Five a.m.

Sighing with relief that my shift was almost over, I stroked the kitty's head and glared at Babe. "We're done now, right?"

Babe held up her fist. "Here's to a successful first night."

I didn't want to, but I gave her a fist bump anyway. With the cat perched on my shoulder, I quickly pulled my car into my driveway. Maybe I'd see Kent before he went to work.

I walked into the house to the aroma of freshly brewed coffee. Just the smell of caffeine alerted my weary senses. I rounded the corner and found Kent in the kitchen. He sat at our breakfast table, about to take a bite of banana bread. He paused with the slice mid-air. "Good morning."

I stared at his hands as my heart beat double-time. "What are you eating?"

"What's that on your shoulder?"

Silence fell as we both stared at each other. Actually, I stared at the bread in his hands, ready to pounce if he started to eat it.

I swallowed, barely noticing the cat clawing at my shoulder again. "You answer first."

Kent held up the bread. "Yeah, I was surprised to find this on the counter this morning. I didn't know you'd baked for me. I can't wait to try it." He raised it to his mouth again.

"No!" In one leap, I bound across the room and smacked the bread from his hands. In the process, I freaked out the cat, which clawed me again before scampering across the room and hiding.

Kent again looked at me like I'd lost my mind. Nothing new. "What is wrong with you? And where did you get that cat?"

I pointed to his breakfast. "I didn't make that bread."

"But it was here on the counter when I woke up." He held out his hands in confusion. I could understand why this was difficult for him. I had no idea how the food had arrived in our kitchen either. "Then someone must have snuck in and left it there. I sure didn't."

Kent walked to the backdoor. Sure enough, the knob was unlocked. "I know I locked this."

I held my hands in the air. "I haven't touched it."

His brows furrowed as he locked the door, hurried past me into the kitchen and lowered himself into the dinette chair. "I don't like this, Laura. What's going on?"

I shrugged, willing my heart rate to slow down to normal, willing my face to not give away my alarm, and willing my life to be anything other than what it had turned out to be. There was so much I wanted to say, yet so much I couldn't. I mean, someone had recorded a conversation inside my house, for goodness sakes! Impulsively, I pushed a button on the radio on my kitchen counter. Rap music filled the room. I cranked it.

"I wish I knew. I just know that someone poisoned Candace and I don't want the same to happen to you."

Kent jerked his head back. "Why would someone want to poison me? And why are we listening to this?"

"New hobby." Was this my opportunity to dig deeper with my husband? I sucked in a breath and met his gaze. I lowered myself across from him at the dinette. "That's a good question. Why would they want to poison you? Maybe it has to do with your work at the pharmacy?"

"Don't be silly. I don't know anything. The police already questioned me yesterday." He held up his coffee. "Is it safe to drink this?" He laughed and took a sip.

Great, he thought I was crazy.

I ignored that and focused on what he'd said before that. "The police questioned you?"

"There were drugs found on the pork rinds. It only makes sense that the police would come to the only pharmacist in town. However, if the person who poisoned Candace came to me, he'd be a few bricks shorts of a stack. I'm sure he or she used one of the pharmacies up in Indy." Kent took another sip of his steaming coffee.

I walked over to the pot and got my own cup. This was definitely a multi-cup morning. I tried to sound casual when I asked, "So, you haven't filled any prescriptions for sleeping pills?"

"Of course I have. Sleeping pills are very common. I can't tell you how many people in town use sleeping pills. You've used sleeping pills."

I ignored the coffee as it burned my tongue. "Who else?"

"I can't tell you that."

He had to be so ethical. Which was the very reason I loved him. He was a man with morals, a near anomaly it seemed sometimes. I leaned against the kitchen counter and collected my thoughts. "I hate to say it, Kent, but I think you know something about Candace's murder, whether you realize it or not. Why else would someone be trying to poison you?"

"Poison me? Someone breaks in and leaves banana bread in our kitchen, and you automatically think I'm being poisoned?"

I realized it did sound rather hasty to someone who hadn't read the threatening note. I shrugged, trying to look nonchalant. "Why else would someone leave banana bread?"

"To be a good neighbor?"

"Good neighbors don't break into homes. They leave cakes and cookies on the doorstep, maybe. They don't barge in. Unless you're Babe, and Babe was with me all night."

He got up and refilled his coffee. "Okay, maybe. But I still think it's over the top to assume the bread is poisoned. And if it is, who says I'm the target? Maybe you know something about Candace's murder that you're not realizing."

"So it makes more sense for someone to be trying to poison me?" I plopped down into the chair across from him. "Besides, how did someone get into our house?"

"We should call the police, I guess. It's a rather odd crime, but with everything that's been happening lately—"

I sighed and pictured Chief Romeo. "They just left."

"What do you mean?"

I explained what happened at the Flynns' and how we ended up with the cat.

Kent shook his head. "Do me a favor? Call the police and let them know what happened. I've got to get ready for work."

※※※

"Did you decide about that couch?"

I swallowed my pride for a moment in order to pretend like I wanted Yvonne's advice. "I don't want the watermelon one. I would like to pick out one for my husband's room."

Her eyes widened and her fingers went to her lips. "He has a separate room? I'm sorry, dear."

I shook my head. "No, not like that. He wants a man cave. You know, a place of his own."

Yvonne let her hand dropped before snickering. "A man cave? Sounds typical. And let me guess—he wants it in time for the Super Bowl?"

Kent hadn't said that, but now that Yvonne mentioned it, maybe getting the room together for the big day was a good idea. It could be my anniversary gift to him. I smiled as I thought about our anniversary. I couldn't wait to see what Kent had planned for us. Every year he surprised me with something—a trip, a romantic date, jewelry. What would he come up with this year? I needed our anniversary to solidify our relationship.

I wandered around until I found the perfect couch for Kent—dark brown leather, soft and comfortable. I could easily see him stretched out across it, relaxing after a hard day of work.

"This is the one!"

Yvonne smiled. "Great! Let's go back to my office and have you fill out the paperwork. It will only take a few minutes."

"Sounds good."

She led me away from the showroom, down a yellow cinder-block hallway and into an overcrowded, outdated office. She pulled out a clipboard from a desk drawer and handed it to me. "I just need some basic information."

I tried to focus on the papers in front of me and resist the urge to let my eyes wander. What kind of clues about Jerry and Candace waited in this office? Had the police already been here to look for evidence? I wanted to snoop, but instead I kept my gaze focused.

Until I heard a bell chime at the front of the store.

Yvonne jerked her head toward the noise. "Listen, I'm the only one working right now—Lou's out to lunch. Can you sit tight a minute?"

Could I ever. "Of course." I watched her leave before lowering the clipboard. My gaze roamed the small space. On a shelf behind the desk, I saw a picture of Jerry, dressed in his kingly attire. There was also a golfing trophy and that gaudy crown he wore in all his commercials.

This was Jerry's office!

My adrenaline surged.

In the distance, I heard Yvonne trying to sell that watermelon-colored couch. Maybe I still had a few minutes before she came back to check on me.

I dodged the desk and plopped into the chair behind it. A calendar was shoved off to the side, covered in papers. Carefully, I slid it out and opened it to January. Various appointments were marked, most of them routine and not helpful. I ran my finger over the week Candace had died. Jerry hadn't marked his South Carolina golf outing there. How strange that he wouldn't put that on his calendar.

Yvonne's voice carried into the office. She was still trying to convince her customers that buying that coral-colored couch would set them apart from everyone else they knew. I couldn't deny the truth in that statement.

Quickly, I opened the top drawer. Nothing except pencils and paper clips.

I opened the next drawer. Beef jerky and candy bars.

Yvonne's voice sounded closer. My heart beat double-time. I couldn't get caught snooping. I eased the drawer shut and propelled myself to the other side of the desk. I grabbed the clipboard just as Yvonne stuck her head back into the office.

"I'll just be another few minutes." Yvonne patted her hair. "Are you okay in here?"

I offered what I hoped to be a sincere-looking smile. "Just fine."

Sweat beaded on my forehead. Tension embedded itself in my neck. But I was fine. Really.

I needed to rinse my moisture-coated face before Yvonne saw me again. Otherwise, she'd know something was up. Being deceitful wasn't exactly my forte.

I stepped into the hallway. To my left was the showroom and the warehouse was to the right. Another office waited at the next door. Candace's, maybe? Surely the police had already checked that out.

There, across the hallway, was a door with a little male and female sign. I'd take a quick trip there to calm my nerves and get myself together.

My shoes fell silently on the floor. I usually preferred heels but these soft little loafers were pretty comfortable and cute to boot.

I twisted the rusty handle and pushed inward, leaning my way into the bathroom as I did so.

A man washed his hands on the other side of the single stall room. I gasped in surprise.

Someone should have locked the door.

Jerry should have locked the door.

# 12

The door slammed in my face. I stood there, nose to nose with the wood, trying to collect my thoughts.

Jerry? Had that really been Jerry?

I might be bored but not enough to make that up.

I gathered my wits before twisting the knob again. I pushed the door open with purpose this time. Sure enough, the man was still at the sink, washing his face.

I stared open-mouthed at my neighbor. He stared back at me with the same expression. Jerry looked like he hadn't slept for days. His comb-over hadn't been combed over. His pasty skin looked even paler with the dark nubs of hair shadowing his jaw. Bags hung like slings under his eyes.

I shut the door behind me and leaned against it. "What are you doing here, Jerry Flynn?

He wiped his face with a paper towel, balled it up, and threw it in the trash with a huff. Water still dripped from his nose.

"Hello? I could use a little privacy." He waved his hands around the small room.

"Don't be ridiculous. You're washing your hands." I scowled. "The police are looking for you."

His expression drooped. "I know."

"What are you doing?"

"Preservation of life." He jabbed his finger into his chest. "I'm hiding."

"If you're hiding, that means you're guilty." I tried to take a step back but the door stopped me. I may have just trapped myself in the bathroom with a killer. I should have at least brought a defense of some sort—a bat, mace, something! If Jerry was capable of killing Candace, he could kill me, and I'd just given him the perfect opportunity.

"No, I'm not guilty. But I look like I am. I know I do. I can't let the police find me. They'll throw me in the slammer."

Which would be exactly where he belonged.

I reached behind me and gripped the doorknob, just to be safe. "When did you get back in town, Jerry?"

He shook his head and the drip of water on his nose flew across the room. "I never went out of town. I've been here the whole time. I swear."

"Listen Jerry, you better start explaining right now, or I'm going to call the cops."

"Keep your voice down!" He patted his hands in the air, as if to say, "hush!" His gaze darted around.

I put a fist to my hip. "Explain."

He scowled before letting out a long sigh. "Okay, okay. I didn't kill my wife. I didn't. I'm devastated at the news."

He didn't look devastated. No, he just looked tired. He probably was tired of running from the law. But did he look like a grieving husband? No way.

I squeezed the door handle, just to make sure I had a good grip in case I needed to jet. "You're supposed to be out of town. That's what Candace told me. That you were golfing."

The little bit of color left on his face drained. "That was just an excuse."

"For what?"

He looked beyond me, as if dreaming of ways to get past me and escape. "For staying here with Yvonne."

My mouth gaped open. "With Yvonne? You mean you two really are having an affair? You jerk."

He at least had the good sense to look sheepish. He even kicked at something imaginary on the floor. "The good news is that I have an alibi."

My hand left the door knob and flew into the air. It didn't stop until my index finger aimed directly at him. "And the bad news is that you're scum. You were cheating on Candace, after all that she's sacrificed for you. How could you? She gave up everything for you."

He shrugged and let his head fall to the side, like the slouch that he was. "I know it's not right. But Candace and I don't love each other. Yvonne's different. We've got chemistry."

I shook my head at his ignorance. "I'm going to have to call the police, Jerry. They're looking for you."

He stepped toward me and I raised my hand in the universal sign for stop.

He paused. "Please don't do it, Laura. I don't want to take the blame for this." His voice trembled. And for a moment—just a small, tiny mark of time—I felt sorry for him.

I wasn't a human lie detector. I didn't know if he killed his wife or not. But this might be my only chance to question him. "I think you care more about your reputation than you do your dead wife."

He shook his head with enough force that I felt a breeze. "It's not true. I hate to think about what happened to Candace. She didn't deserve it. She was a good woman. She put up with me, didn't she?"

Of course he would say that. Candace had supported him from the very beginning, all while he messed around and wasted their money. Why would he want her dead? An insurance policy maybe?

I stared at Jerry, trying to look tougher than I felt. "Any idea who might have done this?"

He looked side to side, as if anyone were close enough to be listening. "Since you asked—Harry McCoy."

I jerked my head back. "Why would you think Harry's guilty?"

"I made him mad a couple of weeks ago. He bought a couch from me, but then found a better deal on another one in Indy. He tried to return it, but I wouldn't let him."

"Why not?"

Jerry shrugged adamantly. "He'd sat on it."

"As do most people when they have couches."

"Anyway, the piece was used goods. Harry got ticked. Threatened me. I bet he went into my house and poisoned those pork rinds, thinking I would eat them. I don't think Candace was supposed to die at all."

I sucked in a deep breath. As someone once said, "oh, what a tangled web we weave." Jerry had woven a doozy.

※※※

"You're sure it was Jerry?" Romeo began his shirt-tucking ritual again. I'd seen him more over the past few days than I had my own husband.

I'd rather see my husband.

"I'm positive. I spoke to him. There's not a large margin for error here." I leaned back on the watermelon couch, suddenly exhausted from all the excitement.

The chief shifted and pulled out his paper and pen. He handed it to Maloney. "Tell me what happened again."

I repeated the story. Again. Chief Romeo nodded, grunted and glanced at Officer Maloney to make sure he was taking notes. Then he looked back at me. "So what happened after he accused Harry?"

I rolled my neck, trying to work out the kinks. "I told Jerry that I was going to call the police, that I had no other choice. As soon as I said that, he pushed past me and ran. I came out of the bathroom in time to see him darting through the warehouse."

Chief Romeo cleaned the front of his teeth with his tongue, in typical Chief Romeo fashion. Thankfully he didn't have any green eggs and ham between them today. "Any idea where he was going?"

I shrugged. "My best guess would be away from you or anyone else who might want to put him behind bars."

Yvonne scowled from the couch across from me. She hadn't been happy that I'd let the cat out of the bag about her affair—or about Jerry's whereabouts. She snarled. "I should have never left you alone."

"It's not my fault Jerry was in the bathroom. I didn't go looking for him." I raised my hands to show my innocence.

Romeo glanced at Yvonne. "We're going to need to take you to the station for questioning."

Yvonne scowled again.

Chief Romeo turned back to me. "If you remember anything else, please let us know." He reached into his pocket, but paused. "I was going to give you my card, but I'm guessing you probably have my number on speed dial by now."

"Ha ha."

His smile slipped. "If you think of anything at all—"

I nodded. If I had a nickel for every time I heard that line, I'd be rich.

※※※

I stopped by the pharmacy on my way home. Jasmine smiled

at me from the front counter. "Hi, Laura, how are you?"

I nodded. I really had no reason to dislike the woman except that she was good-looking and worked with my husband, which seemed awfully insecure. She always seemed perky, and Kent said she was a hard worker. Plus she had no family in the area and apparently had a difficult past. I really should reach out to her more.

"I'm fine, Jasmine. Where's Kent?" I glanced behind her, searching for his figure.

"He had to run a quick errand."

I frowned. "An errand?" As busy as Kent always said he was, it seemed strange he'd be leaving at this time of the day. "Did he say where?"

"Same place he goes every Friday at this time."

I waited for her to continue. When she didn't, I nodded. "Which is?"

She shrugged and carefully placed a label on a prescription bottle. "I have no idea. He always leaves on Fridays at one and returns by two."

I blinked. "Say that again."

"He has some kind of standing appointment every Friday. He doesn't say where." She shrugged and continued working.

How could I not know this? Why would Kent be keeping secrets from me? I felt the wall between us getting higher and thicker. I forced a smile. "Thanks, Jasmine."

Anger, accusations, and hurt continued to build with every turn of my car tires as I drove home. An insanely jealous part of me wanted to drive around town, searching for his car to discover his whereabouts. My logical side concluded that Kent would have a reasonable explanation, that there was nothing to get worried about.

But if there was nothing to get worried about, why was Kent keeping things from me?

But he hadn't been the only one keeping secrets. I had one too. Why did I keep it from Kent? Because there was something to be worried about.

As I pulled into the neighborhood, a group of kids on their bikes created a roadblock as they congregated in the middle of the street. I honked my horn when they didn't move. Couldn't they just be normal and stay inside playing video games?

I gasped at the thought. What was wrong with me? I sounded like Hillary.

I made a mental note that I didn't need to be around her as much, for the simple reason that her self-righteous bossiness might rub off on me.

My shoulders slumped as I pulled into my driveway. I couldn't possibly wait until Kent got home to find out where he'd been. I slouched on the couch and chewed my nails, something I hadn't done since high school. Well, that wasn't true. I had chewed my nails some after "the incident." I thought that, by moving here, I'd forget about it. Yet, it always came to mind at the worst times.

Before I delved too deeply into the memories and hurts, the doorbell rang. Probably Babe again. I welcomed the interruption from my thoughts.

I jerked the door open and saw Tiara standing there with a letter in her hand. "This was in my mailbox."

I held my breath. Another threatening note? Could my day get any worse?

I took the envelope from her and let out the breath I held. Just the water bill. "Thanks, Tiara."

"No problem." She made no effort to move. "I heard you saw Jerry." Tiara looked at me with wide eyes, just begging for a dose of juicy gossip.

I'd take whatever interruption I could get, though I did vow to keep my words in check. Gossiping would only make me feel guilty, which would further push me on my downward spiral. I stepped back and extended my arm. "Come on in. Let me get us coffee."

Coffee always made everything better. I'd never thought so until I moved to Boring.

A few minutes later, I set a mug on the table for her. She sat pertly on the couch with her legs crossed, smiling with her oh-so-white teeth. "So, did Jerry do it?"

I swallowed quickly, trying to appear casual and cool. The hot liquid burned going down my throat, and I sputtered for a moment. So much for appearing cool. "I ran into him at his store."

"And?" She leaned forward and nodded.

I shrugged and gripped my coffee mug. "He says he's not guilty." I wanted to include the fact that Jerry was having an affair, but I didn't. It wasn't my place—although I really wanted to share.

Tiara leaned closer. "I heard the police haven't found him yet, that he disappeared again."

I nodded. "That's the rumor."

"Do you think he did it?"

I shrugged. "It's hard to say." Jerry claimed Harry murdered Candace. I couldn't share that fact either. This gossip thing was really tempting. I sipped my drink to keep my mouth busy and silent.

"Well, I'm just glad you're okay." Tiara patted my knee before picking up her cream-laced coffee again. "You just never know about people these days."

I should take this opportunity to ask her about Donna, to find out what was stressing out Mrs. Prim and Proper. I needed to start shortening my list of suspects. The words were on the tip of my tongue when my doorbell rang again. What was up with people stopping by all the time? Was this typical for small-town America?

I opened the door and saw Donna there, cookies in hand. "I saw Tiara stop by. You guys can't have a pow-wow without me!" She laughed, though the high-pitch chuckle made her seem nervous. I wondered what Donna had to be nervous about?

"Come on in."

She shoved the cookies into my hands as she joined Tiara on the couch.

I poured her a mug of coffee and heard Tiara filling her in

while I did so.

"That's just awful, Laura," Donna said, sitting with her legs crossed at the ankles and hands folded over her knees. I wondered if she'd ever done any beauty pageants. She seemed the type.

I set her coffee on the table. "I know. It is awful. I can't believe all of this has happened in our neighborhood."

Tiara shook her head. "I hope they catch that no-good loser."

I cleared my throat. Though I didn't want to do it, I knew I needed to change the subject. "So, what's new with you two?"

They both shrugged, as if the subject change disappointed them. Silence reigned for a moment, as if any other topic of conversation left them mystified.

"We're getting new carpet," Tiara offered.

"Matthew got first place in the spelling bee at school," Donna said.

We went through our usual chitchat about clothes and TV shows and happenings about town. When silence fell, Donna turned an inquisitive gaze on me.

"So, how do you like your new role as a housewife? It's a big change from having a nine-to-five job, isn't it?" She sipped her drink, peering at me as she waited for my response.

"It sure is." That was my understatement of the year. I'd give anything to be working as publicist for J.W. and Associates again. All those designer clothes I used to wear to work were just going to waste. Not to mention all my time.

"Is Kent enjoying his new job?" Donna blinked and waited

for my answer.

Enjoying the job more than me. "Yes, he seems to be."

"I wish my husband enjoyed his job." Tiara tapped her extra-long manicured fingernails on the arms of the chair. "All he ever does is complain. And then he's so tired when he gets home. He just wants to watch TV and veg out. I remember the days when we'd go out on the town, when we'd sit beside each other on the couch and snuggle. Now we each have our own chairs."

"It's happens to every good marriage," Donna said matter-of-factly.

"It sure does," Tiara agreed.

I leaned forward, nearly holding my breath with anticipation. "What does? What happens to every good marriage?" What did they know that I didn't?

"Every good marriage grows stale," Tiara said. "It's just a part of life. We're in the winter stage."

"But you're only in your thirties!"

"It's not a matter of age, sweetie. It just happens after the newness wears off. Habit and routine sets in. Priorities change. Kids come along." She shrugged nonchalantly, as if she'd just announced a menu selection. "It's just life."

"But spring always comes after the winter, right?" I couldn't believe that my marriage was doomed to be like this for good. This had to be just a phase.

Donna and Tiara looked at each other for a split-second. Then Donna shrugged again. "Sometimes. You think it's bad now, you just wait until you have kids. He stops seeing you as a woman and starts seeing you as a mom." She sighed ever-so-briefly, and I thought for sure she wasn't as laid-back about this conversation as she tried to appear. "But, like Tiara said, it's just life. You've got to roll with it."

Maybe we shouldn't have kids, then. My mind raced with a million thoughts, all of them near panic-stricken.

"Oh, Tiara. We're scaring the poor girl. She obviously thinks marriage is much better than it is." Donna laughed, but it sounded brittle. Then she sighed. "So, has anyone heard when Candace's funeral will be?"

I was grateful for the subject change, even if it meant going back to the topic of murder. "It's Monday, I heard."

"Who's organized it? I mean, with Jerry being MIA and all?" Tiara asked.

"The community church did. I guess Candace was an only child, and both of her parents are deceased. With Jerry out of the picture, the church stepped up." Someone had called me today and asked if I could make a casserole for the reception afterward. I said yes, of course. Now I had to figure out what I could make that would edible for that many people. The last thing we needed was another murder in town, this one thanks to my cooking.

Tiara glanced at her watch. "I've got to run, ladies. My spinning class starts in thirty."

I leaned forward, my interest sparked. "Where do you take spinning?"

"Over at the gym. If you want to call it a gym. It's really just two rooms—one with weights, and one for the occasional exercise class. There's usually hardly anyone in there. Aside from Harry. Harry's always there."

Harry? Suddenly, I felt energy return to me. "I've been wanting to try out spinning."

Tiara waved her hand in the air, beckoning me to follow. "You should come then. The first class is free."

# 13

The gym in Boring was really just an old gas station that had several weight machines and a treadmill. I'd never done a spinning class before, but I had seen it done on TV. How hard could it be?

My eyes scanned the place as I walked in. Across the room, on a machine that looked more like a torture device, sat a heaving and huffing Harry. I watched him a moment. Could he be the killer? Or was Jerry just trying to throw me off his trail? I mean, a couch is a pretty trivial thing to commit murder over. I suppose people had committed crimes because of less, though.

A window separated the spinning room from the weight equipment. That meant that while my legs went round and round, I could also keep an eye on Harry, see if he acted suspicious.

"You need to get warmed up first," Tiara said. "You know, stretch out."

I glanced through the window at Harry, still working

diligently with a weight machine that made his muscles bulge. I'm sure that was the effect he was going for. I noticed a couple other females in the class eyeing him.

"He likes to show off for the ladies," Tiara whispered, all the while pulling her leg nearly over her head. How did she bend that way?

I tried to copy her and nearly tumbled onto my face. I'd stick with something more basic—I reached for my toes, but only got to my knees. I never was the athletic type; I left that to Kent.

Speaking of Kent—I glanced at my watch. It was dinnertime. I wondered if he'd be home on time today. I needed to ask him where he went every Friday. I'd been so mad that I didn't even bother to leave him a note to say where I was.

Maybe our marriage was going south. Maybe Donna and Tiara were right, and I should just give in to the inevitable routine of a stale marriage.

"Laura! Great to have you here. Your first time doing a spinning class?" A neighbor, Karen Jones, who lived two streets over approached me, looking very fit and trim in her exercise outfit.

"No, I've never done spinning before." How hard could it be? I just had to ride an exercise bike for thirty minutes, right?

Karen patted my hand. "I'll try and take it easy on you, then." She grinned. What did that mean?

As I climbed onto my stationary bike, I glanced back over to where Harry was.

His machine was empty.

My gaze flew across the gym. I didn't see him anywhere. Where did he go?

"Okay, let's start this slow, ladies. Let's go nice and easy to get warmed up."

I turned the pedals round and round. Already, my behind hurt from the impossibly small seat.

"You doing okay, Berry?"

I glanced at my instructor, horrified that she'd called me out. "Just fine, thanks."

I tried to pay attention as we went up hills and raced in an imaginary bike run and then went up and down several more hills.

Sweat poured down my brow.

I glanced back out at the weight machines. Still no Harry. Did he leave? Where could he have gone?

"I need your full attention, Berry. Spinning takes concentration."

I snapped my gaze back to Karen—who, now that I thought about it, used to be a drill sergeant in the army. Convenient.

Why did everyone else in the class look like they were enjoying it? Riding these bikes was torture, pure and simple. The other participants were smiling despite the sweat dripping down their faces. A few even cheered on occasion. They were obviously all freaks.

I tried to keep my head facing Karen and let my eyes look to the side. A moment later, Harry emerged from the nook where the bathrooms and water fountain were located, sipping a paper cup of water and talking to someone.

The Godfather.

My new neighbor, whose name escaped me at that moment.

The conversation didn't look lighthearted and fun. There weren't any smiles or laughing eyes. Harry scanned the room, as if to make sure there were no listening ears or watching eyes.

Then he slipped something out of his pocket and handed it to the Godfather.

Could Harry have paid him to knock off Candace?

"How you doing, Berry?"

Karen's voice snapped me back to reality. Suddenly, my legs began moving in circles and I couldn't stop them. My thighs burned. My calves were crying out. My gluteus maximus demanded a break.

Before I could convince them otherwise, my muscles went as limp as spaghetti and I sprawled across the floor.

※※※

"Spinning class, huh? I never thought you'd be interested in something like that." Kent placed another compress on my knee, which had rammed into the bike on my way to the ground.

"What better time than now to get into shape?" I tried to bend my other leg and grimaced. Man, were my muscles sore. Already. That wasn't a good sign.

"It's a good thing Tiara could bring you home. I don't think you could have driven in your current state."

"I'll be fine. I just need to let my muscles recover."

"You pushed yourself too hard. Karen Jones feels terrible. She's called three times to check on you."

"I scowled. "Karen Jones is a Nazi. She delighted in torturing me."

Kent smiled. "I'm sure that's not true."

"Oh, but it is. That class was just awful."

"Hopefully the pain reliever will kick in soon." Kent sat across from me. "In the meantime, why don't you tell me about your day? Anything exciting happen?"

"I ran into Jerry Flynn. Does that count?"

"I thought I'd heard rumor of such."

"Working in the pharmacy, I guess you get to hear everything." You would have heard it directly from me, but you weren't there when I stopped by. I don't know why I didn't voice my thoughts aloud. Maybe I wasn't ready to face reality if I didn't like his answer.

"I can't believe he was hiding in town this whole time."

"I can't believe he was having an affair. I mean, how do people get to that point in their marriage?"

"They don't respect their vows. They don't feel their partner is making them happy anymore, so they look for someone who can. We were talking about this at our last men's Bible study. When you first get married, you concentrate on making the other person happy. After awhile, it becomes about your spouse making you happy. The truth of the matter is that happiness comes from within."

"Food for thought." I questioned my own understanding of

our relationship. Where did I stand on the happiness issue?

Kent kissed my forehead. "Not everyone has it as good as we do."

Did we have it good? Did Kent really think that? Couldn't he see how we were drifting apart lately?

There was one thing I knew: I, Laura Berry, wasn't happy. And I had to do something about my current mental state. Soon.

# 14

The scent of apple pies, cinnamon, and other sweet somethings drifted through the air. If I let myself, I could easily gain five pounds today.

It was Saturday, the day of the church bake sale. In Boring, this was apparently the event of the year. A quartet sang over in one corner of the church's fellowship hall. All around the perimeter were tables with various treats. All the pies were together, as well as cakes, cookies, brownies, candy and, of course, the breads.

Any of the food could be poisoned, I rationalized. After all, each piece was homemade. All someone had to do was slip a little something in with the flour and sugar.

I also realized that if I could find the banana bread, I might find the killer.

As I stood behind my table, I carefully scanned all the goodies. Since I didn't bake, I promised to man a section.

As soon as I got the chance, I'd make my way to that table with the banana bread. Emma Jean was manning that section and I didn't want to cause any trouble. I'd gotten stuck selling the pies.

Things were hopping much more than I'd anticipated, and we'd had a steady crowd since we opened our doors. There was a killer out there, and here we were selling homemade foods. The thought disturbed me, but I was sure if I mentioned it, people would find me paranoid.

The one thing about the bake sale was that everyone from town came out for it. I'd met several new people and many had offered their condolences to me since I found Candace. I also heard several theories from people eager to share. They said it was because I was now a member of the Neighborhood Watch.

One person said someone killed Candace because she and Jerry were involved in a Star Trek role playing game that went too far.

Another person said Candace had put the sleeping pills on those pork rinds herself. It was suicide.

Still another person claimed Jerry wanted to cash in on his wife's life insurance policy. I'd heard that one several times now. Maybe these people were on to something.

"Laura, I was hoping to find you here."

Hillary stood at my table wearing a smart navy blue suit. Come to think of it, I never saw her not wearing a suit.

"Hi, Hillary." I held up a pie. "Would you like to buy a pie? Part of the money is going toward Candace's funeral."

"Not now." Her voice sounded serious. "I need your help."

"Sure, what's going on?"

"I can't talk about it here. Can you meet me tonight?"

Kent's face flashed in my mind. I'd really wanted to spend some time with him, maybe figure out what was going on.

"I'm desperate, Laura."

I supposed Kent and I could talk later. "Sure, Hillary. Where do you want to meet?"

"My house. Five o'clock. Sound good?"

"I'll be there."

I watched as she briskly walked away, and wondered what had her so upset. I guess I'd find out tonight.

"Hi, Lauren."

I glanced up and saw my new neighbor. "Hi, Gia. How are you?"

"I just thought I'd come and check out this little sale I've heard so much about." She looked around the church in disdain.

"We have lots of goodies." I studied her a moment, realizing she wasn't interested in any of the food. She seemed preoccupied with something else as she glanced around the building. I cleared my throat. "Are you all moved in?"

She swung her gaze back toward me and twirled a lock of hair, looking bored. "We're getting there. I'm so tired of moving."

"You've moved a lot, huh?"

She shrugged. "You could say that. Hopefully we'll be here for awhile." She looked around again. "Or maybe not."

"Boring takes getting used to."

Her eyebrows flickered up. "You could say that."

I glanced around the room. "No husband with you today?"

"No, he's working."

"What does he do for a living again?"

She seemed to hesitate. "We're business owners."

This would be a great time for me to practice being neighborly. "Oh, do you? What kind of business?"

Her gaze met mine. "We sell futons."

※※※

I couldn't stop thinking about Gia's confession. Okay, it wasn't so much a confession, but to me, that's what it sounded like. I mean, a futon store? Why here in Boring, of all places? I mean, we already had a store dedicated entirely to couches.

Could it be motive for murder?

Lately, it seemed like everyone had a motive.

Maybe even my own husband. I mean, he was keeping secrets from me. I had no idea what he could be doing that he wouldn't tell me about. All I knew was that it equaled trouble. I bit my lip.

I still needed to wander to the bread table. We'd close everything down at two p.m., which was only an hour and a half away. I asked the woman beside me if she'd keep an eye on my table for a minute. She agreed.

I meandered around the tables, trying to appear casual and like I wasn't making a beeline for Emma Jean. I made polite conversation as I went, and I eventually stopped to look at the breads.

Emma Jean scowled as she held out a loaf bundled in green plastic wrap. "Would you like some delicious treats, made by our wonderful locals?" she asked with her scratchy, slightly grating and way-too-loud voice.

I rubbed my hands together and offered a polite smile. "I'm looking for banana bread. Any of that over here?"

"No, it sold out this morning. Very popular. Very, very popular."

I snapped my fingers. "That's too bad. Do you know who made it? Maybe I can get the recipe from her?"

"The same person who makes it every year."

I waited for that person's name. When Emma Jean didn't offer, I asked, "And who would that be?"

"The former homecoming queen of Boring High, class of 1988. A respected member of the community. A dear friend, great mom and dedicated wife."

Again, I waited. Emma Jean had to point out that the person was an "original." It was her way of letting me know that I wasn't a part of Boring's inner circle. That was Emma Jean for you. I tapped my foot, losing patience. "A name, please."

Emma Jean smirked. "Donna, of course."

❈❈❈

Donna couldn't be a killer. Not Mrs. Suzy Homemaker, the former cheerleader with her football star husband. The two had been high school sweethearts but went their separate ways during college. They both married other people but then got divorced. They reconnected several years back, and had been together ever since.

But Harry did say that Donna and Candace had been arguing on the day before she died. I had to find out about the bad blood between them.

As soon as I got home, I'd make a list of my suspects. I just couldn't keep them straight anymore, not when it seemed like everyone in town had some sort of motive.

When the bake sale ended, I quickly collected my things and hurried home. The TV blared in the background as I walked into the house. I found my husband in the living room reclining on the couch and munching on popcorn. The microwavable bags seemed safe enough, though everything was suspect in my mind lately.

"Did you bring me back anything from the bake sale?" Kent stretched across the couch, his sock-clad feed propped up on the arm. Football played on the TV. Thank goodness he didn't drink. Otherwise, he might just be the stereotypical couch potato.

I nearly gasped at the thought. Maybe that was our problem ... both of us were becoming stereotypes. He was becoming the couch potato. I was becoming the overbearing wife. And our marriage was suffering from the mythical seven-year itch.

"Laura?"

My gaze refocused on Kent. "Yes?"

"Did you bring me anything from the bake sale? Maybe

some cannoli like I requested?"

Was he kidding? No way was I buying anything at that sale. Who knew what people could have put in those baked goods.

"Nope, sure didn't."

He sat up slightly and looked at me with a knot between his eyes. "Why not?"

"We don't need anything. Otherwise, we'll both get the middle-age bulge. No one wants that."

"I've never known you to be so concerned for your weight, Laura, until recently." He stuffed more popcorn in his mouth.

"It's never too early to start thinking about living a healthy lifestyle."

"Of course." He muted the game. "So, what's going on for the rest of the day?"

I sat down beside him. "I don't know. I was hoping maybe you had some ideas."

He shrugged, his attention drawn back to the silent TV screen. Suddenly, he was on his feet, and the popcorn scattered over the floor. "Yes! Did you see that play? Did you see it? It was incredible. I just can't believe it."

I slowly blew out the breath I held. "Nope, I missed it, sorry to say."

"I can't believe it." His fist looped in the air. "Yes! A touchdown. Laura, that was just amazing."

"Sounds like it."

I thought about picking up the popcorn but decided against it. He made the mess; he could clean it up.

Finally, he calmed down enough to see kernels all over the floor. He knelt to pick them up. "That was just unbelievable."

"You mentioned that." I couldn't keep the irritation out of my voice. He didn't seem to notice.

Finally, he looked at me again. "So, what were we talking about again?"

"Our plans for tonight."

"Oh, right. I figured we'd just stay home and take it easy. I'm exhausted from working so much lately. I really don't want to do anything."

I wasn't surprised, but I was disappointed. When would things ever return to normal? Or was this our new normal?

It was just as well. I excused myself—which Kent hardly noticed because the game came back on—and went into our office area. I pulled out a notebook and jotted down all of my thoughts.

I made a list of all the possible suspects, starting with Donna. Beside her name, I wrote: seen arguing with Candace. Homeowners' Association? Banana bread?

Then I wrote Jerry: Life insurance policy?

Yvonne: To be with Jerry?

Harry: Angry about couch?

Gia: Opening a competitive store?

Kent? I didn't have a motive to write beside my husband's name, which was just as well. Still, I couldn't ignore the secrets he'd been hiding lately.

Next, I wrote down my clues. My first was the threatening

note. Someone had to put it in my mailbox without being noticed. I suppose anyone on my street could have done it, but Donna was the most likely. Then there was the banana bread. That seemed most likely to be Donna also.

I still couldn't believe she would be capable of killing Candace. Besides, I didn't have a reasonable motive for her.

What other clues was I missing?

There were the poisoned pork rinds, of course. Someone had to get into the Flynns' house to poison the pork rinds, and that same person had to have access to sleeping pills. According to Kent, anyone could have gotten the drug because so many people used it.

What was I missing?

The phone rang and I snatched it up.

"Hey, chickaroonie. Did you hear the news?"

I perched the phone under my ear to talk to Babe. "What news?"

"The police found Jerry."

# 15

Now that I could stop thinking about Candace's murder, I could fully focus on other worthy pursuits—like meeting with Hillary. I had no idea what she wanted to talk to me about, but meeting with her beat staying home to watch my husband watch TV. I had to keep myself busy, keep my mind occupied with things other than my failures.

"I've got to run over and meet with Hillary for a little while, okay, Kent?" I slipped on my coat, glancing over my shoulder to see the TV flickering as a commercial flashed on the screen. The back of my husband's head bobbed up and down as he laughed at whatever antic the marketing guru had developed to keep his attention. It worked. My husband didn't even look back at me.

"No problem." He threw a piece of popcorn in the air and caught it in his mouth. "I'll just be here vegging out."

Of that, I had no doubt. "Vegging out" was a phrase I'd been hearing a lot lately. I was beginning to hate the term.

Again, I bundled up in my coat, hat and scarf to go to Hillary's place. She answered the door before I ever rang the bell. Her husband was out of town again, looking for more land to develop. He seemed to be gone more than he was here. I'd only met him once, and he'd seemed likable enough. I guessed it was true that opposites did attract.

Lines of worry still etched Hillary's face. "Come in."

I stepped out of the cold. "How are you?"

"Not well. Thanks for coming."

I braced myself. At this point, there was no telling what she might say. The thought briefly fluttered through my mind—what if it involved Kent somehow? Would I really want to hear it?

Scenarios had been going through my mind for awhile now. What could a pharmacist be involved with? Selling prescription drugs to those without a prescription, for one. What if that's what Kent was doing? What if he had a noble reason, like he did it for people who couldn't afford their medications? But still, it would be illegal. He could go to jail.

Or even worse, what if he was having an affair? No, I couldn't believe it. But affairs had happened to even the most unlikely couples. One could never be too cocky.

"I don't know how to say this, Laura."

My heart raced. "Just say it, Hillary. It's okay." But was it? Would this moment change my life forever?

Hillary's face contorted, like her inner pain had gotten the best of her. I braced myself.

"Donna is going to run against me for president of the

association!" She broke into sobs and buried her face in her hands.

I let her words sink in. That's what this was about? I wanted to laugh, but I didn't. Instead, I patted her shoulder. I'd never seen Hillary show an ounce of emotion until now. "It's going to be okay, Hillary. You're an experienced leader."

She glanced up from her hands. "You think so?"

Experienced was the nicest way I could say it. "Yes, you're very experienced. Everyone values that."

She sniffled. "Thanks, Laura. I needed to hear that. I've worked so hard to get where I am."

"You have. Your tenacity has inspired a lot of people, I'm sure."

"I only want what's best for the neighborhood. All I've ever wanted to do was to be a leader. It's the reason I went to Brown."

I stopped patting her shoulder. "You went to Brown?"

She nodded. "I had big dreams."

"What happened?"

"I think I married the wrong person."

My eyes widened. "Mark seems like a nice man."

"He doesn't support my dreams. So, instead of running for city council, I'm forced to focus all my energies on this Homeowners' Association. I've found my calling here."

In one way, it was good to know Kent and I weren't the only couple that struggled with issues. Sometimes, that's what it felt like. On the other hand, was anyone really happy?

"Does Mark support you here?"

She shrugged. "I suppose. He's gone so much that it really doesn't matter. Now that the kids are teenagers, he pretty much lets me do my own thing."

"Is he building another neighborhood somewhere?"

"On the other side of Indy. The housing market here seems to have dried up. I expect it to surge again, though. It's just a matter of time. People are going to be coming to Boring in droves one day. It's the type of small town that everyone wants to be a part of."

"I'm sure it is." But not if the townsfolk had anything to say about it.

Hillary shook her head. "Please, have a seat, Laura. I'm sorry you had to see that meltdown. I've been under a great deal of stress lately."

"Is everything okay?"

She looked at me with her red eyes. Her hands shook as she wiped a strand of hair behind her ear. "That's why I asked you to come over, actually. I need your help."

"Sure, Hillary. What can I help you with?" I couldn't imagine what she needed my help with.

Her gaze stayed on mine and for the first time, I saw a touch of softness in her eyes. Amazing.

"Laura, you just seem to have everything so together. I need someone like you on my side."

Was she asking me to be her friend? I wasn't confident about where this conversation was going. In fact, I felt downright confused.

Hillary drew in a deep breath. "Laura, I need you to help me with my campaign. Donna may be my most fierce competition yet."

"People have run against you before?"

"Of course. It wouldn't be much of a victory if I ran unopposed."

"Of course," I repeated. Unease rose in me. "This is an awkward position I'm in, Hillary."

"Donna wants to amend the bylaws." Her voice rose in outrage. "She wants to put a limit on how many terms I can serve. She's just doing it so she can win." Hillary's brows formed one long line across her forehead. The line matched the wrinkles on her brow.

"Most positions do have term limits."

"I'm the best person for this job!" Hillary stood, her face red. Her manic expression vanished as quickly as it appeared. "I am the best person, Laura. I care about this neighborhood. After all, my husband built it. I have a personal stake in everyone here. I know people think I'm strict, but I have to be."

I tried to keep my voice soft. "Hillary, I'm Donna's friend as well."

"I know. But you know I'm a better president than she would ever be. You know I am, Laura."

The truth was, I didn't know that.

"Hillary, what do you want me to do?"

"I want you to help preserve this neighborhood, that's what. Donna wants to ease the rules of the association. Do you know what that would cause?"

"I guess I don't."

She grabbed my arm. "Come. Let me show you."

She led me outside and into her car. The next thing I knew, she'd cranked the engine and took off toward the outskirts of town. She drove silently, which was the last thing I needed. My thoughts turned over again and again as I tried to figure out how not to hurt someone's feelings. Joining Hillary's camp would probably end my friendship with Donna. Truth be told, I didn't know who would be the better president. Hillary drove me crazy sometimes—most of the time, for that matter—but at least she stayed on top of things. Donna probably would too. I did not want to be in this position.

When Hillary drove out of Boring, northward toward Indianapolis, and kept going for forty-five minutes, I got nervous. Finally, she turned into a subdivision filled with vinyl-sided homes and saplings that were barely visible in the nighttime sky.

I glanced at the houses around me, perplexed. Of all the places I thought she might take me, this was not one of them. "Hillary, what are we doing here?"

She braked and spread her hands wide. Her headlights illuminated the area ahead of us. "You see this subdivision?"

How could I miss it? "It's dark, but yes. Kind of."

"It's only ten years old. Ten years." She began driving again and turned down a side street. The homes themselves looked similar to the ones in our neighborhood, just not as well maintained. She stopped by a house on the corner and pointed at a house with a chain-link fence, something that wasn't allowed in our neighborhood.

"Look, do you see those tomato cages in the backyard?"

I squinted. "Sort of."

"The owner sits outside in the summertime and watches his plants grow all day. Then he leaves the evidence of his sloppy gardening up all year for everyone who passes to see it."

We drove to the next street.

"You see that house on the corner? The man who lives there has homing pigeons. They fly around the neighborhood and mess on everyone's cars. And that house? It has a deck—in the front! And these people? They planted fake trees in their yard. Fake trees!"

She continued on with her soliloquy, waxing eloquently on the evils of a neighborhood with no rules.

"This could be our neighborhood if Donna is in charge, Laura. Do you want this?"

I could admit that the place didn't look as nice as Dullington Estates but, listening to Hillary, you'd think it was the ghetto. "How do you know about this neighborhood, Hillary? Why did you bring me here, of all places?"

"Because I used to live here. Finally, the chaos just got to be too much to bear. I knew I needed a place to live with structure, where the American dream could be reality again." I thought I saw the gleam of tears in her eyes.

"Why are you so sure Donna would let things go downhill?"

Hillary slammed on the brakes and looked at me. "Because Donna has a criminal record, that's why."

I gasped. "Donna? How do you know that?"

Hillary's unwavering gaze never left me. "Because Candace told me before she died."

❀❀❀

"Why do you look like you're beside yourself?" Kent slipped a striped tie around the collar of his starched white shirt as he dressed for church the next day.

I shrugged as I jammed my earring in place. "I don't know. I'm fine."

Kent continued to look in the mirror as he looped his tie into a knot. "Ever since you got together with Hillary last night, you haven't acted like yourself."

I shrugged again, not that Kent was looking. "I just have a lot on my mind."

"Like what?" Finally, he glanced at me. But just as quickly, he was back to adjusting his tie.

I considered what to say to him before settling on, "Hillary wants me to help with her campaign, which I'm sure would put my friendship with Donna in jeopardy. I don't know what to do."

His tie must have looked satisfactory, because he grabbed his sports coat and slid his arms through. "Maybe you shouldn't help with either. Just stay out of it."

It sounded like a simple enough solution.

He wrapped his arms around me from behind—just what I'd been wanting. Before I found out he was keeping secrets from me, at least. "Anything else on your mind?"

Tension squeezed my shoulders. Was this the time to bring up his secret? No, I decided. Not before church. We had to leave soon or we'd be late—and Kent hated to be late. "No. Should there be?"

He shrugged and released me. "I guess not."

"There's not."

Kent offered his arm. "Okay then. Ready for church?"

"Let's go." I looped my arm in his.

We walked in to Boring Community Church. Thankfully, the church didn't live up to its name. I mean, sure, Kent and I were two of the youngest members in the congregation of a hundred, the music was slow, and the sermons were less than inspiring. Despite those minor details, the church was one of the best things about my move here—maybe the only good thing, for that matter.

The people were welcoming, the food good, and the faith steady. We slipped into the pew.

Harry stood in front of us.

I'd never seen him at church before. Maybe he felt the need to be here for the forgiveness of sins. Had he killed Candace? He seemed more like the type who'd kill someone with his hands instead of using poison. Apparently, he could be a hothead sometimes. Someone had smothered her, but other details had been carefully plotted.

I had to stop. Even at church I couldn't stop thinking about murder or suspecting people of being killers.

Forgive me, Lord.

The pastor talked about gossip, which I thought was appropriate. I couldn't help but feel he was speaking directly to me. In fact, it even seemed his eyes kept focusing on me. I shifted in the pew and looked down at my sermon outline.

I knew gossip was wrong. I knew I shouldn't be speculating so much lately about my neighbors. But how would I crack this case if I didn't ask questions? Why was gossip such a struggle? Why was it so easy to justify?

"You okay?" Kent whispered.

I nodded. But was I? Maybe God was disappointed with me. Maybe He was more than disappointed—maybe He was angry.

God didn't like gossip. I'd learned that from the moment I started going to church.

So I guess I just had to learn to keep my mouth shut—all the while trying to find a killer.

※※※

Tiara and her husband, Darius, came over for a cookout after church. Kent had invited them, mostly because Darius also rooted for the Chicago Bears, and Kent wanted to talk football with someone.

It wasn't that I minded the couple coming over. Tiara was pleasant enough, even if her best friend was a killer.

Possibly.

Or was it Harry? Or Jerry?

I needed to let the suspects percolate in my mind for awhile longer. I felt sure I could figure things out, if just given the right amount of time. The problem was, time wasn't on my side. Not when a killer wanted my neck on the chopping block.

Kent and Darius, along with the twins, were outside on the deck overlooking the lake, grilling chicken and steak while Tiara and I prepared pasta salad inside. Maybe this would be a good time to ask Tiara some questions about Donna—strictly on a factual level. No gossip.

"How's Donna been doing lately? She's seemed a little stressed." I licked my lips, hoping I didn't sound too eager.

Tiara shrugged and continued to chop celery. "She's just been busy, I guess."

"I'm sure it's stressful running for president of the Homeowner's Association."

Her head jerked toward me. "You know about that?"

I nodded. "Hillary's a pretty fierce opponent."

"She's controlling, that's what she is. Someone needs to put her in her place."

"I never knew that Donna had an interest in running for office." I tried to sound casual as I cut up a couple tomatoes and added EVOO—extra virgin olive oil.

"Someone's gotta step up and take a stand against Hillary." Tiara looked at me. "I mean, you think so, too, right? Or has Hillary cast her spell over you?"

I found myself at a loss for words. "Hillary is a bit overbearing."

"You should join Donna's campaign then."

I opened my mouth but nothing came out.

Thankfully, Kent stuck his head in the back door. "How much longer, ladies?"

"About ten minutes!" I called back. I quickly mixed the rest of the ingredients, hoping the subject of Donna's campaign would be forgotten. No such luck.

We decided to eat on the deck since the day was unseasonably warm. We settled at the table and adjusted the umbrella to block the sun from our eyes. The charred remains of our shed stood in the distance, a visible reminder of the threat my little family was under. Kent and Darius seemed oblivious to it as they chatted about how to get rid of crabgrass.

If only that was my biggest worry.

A moment of silence fell as we all dug into our food.

"So, who do you think did it?" Darius sliced his steak and put a hefty bite in his mouth. As he chewed, he looked each of us in the eye.

"He's so obsessed with the whole mess!" Tiara said, throwing her hand in the air and laughing. "I think he wants to be Columbo or something."

"There's a killer on the loose in Boring. Everyone should be obsessed with it."

I nodded. "He's right."

His dark eyes connected with mine. "So, what's your theory?"

Donna, Harry, Yvonne? Who did I start with?

I remembered that sermon about gossip. I should start with no one, I realized, with a slight slump to my shoulders. "I have no idea. I wish the police would arrest someone and soon. Or I wish Jerry would just confess."

I was willing to let the subject drop. Sure, I wanted to ask for more opinions, but I would be the good girl.

"Well, I think it's Harry." Darius raised his eyebrows as if waiting for a reaction.

I nearly choked on my water, which then turned into a cough attack. Kent pounded my back, looking at me with scrunched eyebrows.

Tiara stared at her husband with wide eyes. "Darius! That's not very nice."

"Neither is murder."

Tiara held her palm to the sky and shook her head. "It's so ridiculous. He thinks Harry did it because he used to date Candace."

I coughed again. "Harry and Candace used to date?"

Tiara wrinkled her nose. "I thought everyone knew that. We all thought they'd get married one day."

"What happened?" The question slipped out before I could stop it.

"They went away to college, and Candace dumped him for Jerry."

"Jerry went to college?"

"Laura!" It was Kent's turn to reprimand me this time.

"I didn't mean that he doesn't seem educated. It's just that–" Okay, so that was exactly what I'd meant.

"They didn't meet in class. Jerry delivered pizzas to her

college dorm. That's how they met," Tiara offered.

I wanted to look at Kent and say, "See! I was right." I restrained myself.

"Were you around when they opened the store? What's it been? Ten years now?" I wiped my mouth with a napkin.

Darius nodded. "Candace was working in finance up in Indianapolis. Jerry convinced her to give up her job to support his dream of opening a furniture store. I don't think she ever forgave him."

"I wonder why he wanted to open a couch store, of all things."

"He certainly knew all about couches—that's where he spent most of his time." Tiara laughed and I found myself giggling, too. I knew I shouldn't. But what she said was true: If anyone knew about couches, it was Jerry.

"I guess the store never really took off?" Kent asked, wiping his mouth. I raised my eyebrows, surprised he had any interest.

"The store probably could have done okay, but the right leadership just wasn't in place," Darius said. "Candace tried to manage the business side of things, but Jerry just kept spending money on those stupid commercials. He wanted his fifteen minutes of fame."

I remembered his commercials and winced. I sure wouldn't want to be known as the man who wore tights and a cape. But that was just me.

Darius shrugged, and speared a piece of pasta. "Who knows? Maybe he did kill Candace. I wouldn't put it past him."

# 16

A couple of hours later, we all relaxed on the deck with ice cream sundaes. The sun crept toward the horizon, and the unusually warm weather was a welcome relief from the frigid days we'd had lately.

One thing I did like about Boring was this deck. I liked the view of the lake and the sounds of the geese honking. I even liked being able to catch a glimpse of the luscious green golf course in the distance.

I never had this in Chicago. I had a balcony overlooking an alley instead.

"Toby! Get back here. Jack, those geese will bite you!"

Tiara abandoned her ice cream to chase her three-year-old twins. As she grabbed them both in a hug, Darius leaned close to us. "I could just look at her all day. She's even more beautiful now than on the day we met."

I looked over at Tiara. She was beautiful, no one could deny that. And when I looked at Darius looking at her, my heart lurched. Kent used to look at me that way.

And I used to not feel sorry for myself like I had lately.

Still, I couldn't help but think that other couples had something that Kent and I didn't. Or something that Kent and I had lost.

I glanced at Kent. He and Darius were already talking about the Bears.

My heart sagged even further.

I looked at the sky. Lord, can't I be successful in at least one area of my life? You stripped me of my career and ambitions. Now I'm feeling like a failure in my marriage. And even something simple like investigating a murder—okay, maybe it's not really that simple, but it still leaves me coming up short. I just need a small touch of hope, a sign that things will get better.

"Are you okay?" Kent whispered. I looked over and saw both men staring at me.

I nodded. "Just looking for rainbows."

※※※

That evening, I asked Babe if she'd like to take a walk. Maybe talking with my friend would help clear my mind. Everything seemed out of focus lately: my marriage, my relationship with God, my relationships in general. I knew from the uneasiness in my gut that I needed to change something in my life. I just wasn't sure what.

The sun had already set when Babe and I began strolling the neighborhood. The whole subdivision was lined with sidewalks, which made it ideal for long jaunts. Some of the houses circled the lake and others were flush up against the golf course. There were no noisy sounds of highways or construction or people partying too late.

Maybe I was beginning to like it here in Boring after all. I didn't miss those old aspects of my life in the least.

I kicked a rock out of my way on the sidewalk, in no hurry to get anywhere. I tried to think of small talk to start with, before jumping into the deeper issues. Babe must have sensed my anxiety because, for once, she remained quiet. She almost had a faraway look in her eyes.

"Are the police going to let Jerry come to the funeral tomorrow?" I asked, still chasing the rock with my foot as it scampered ahead of me.

"That's what I heard through the neighborhood scuttlebutt. The five-Os don't have enough evidence to charge him."

"Five-Os?"

"You know, the PoPo."

"PoPo?"

"The police, Laura. The police. Get with it." She snapped her fingers.

"Not enough evidence? He lied. He had an affair. That seems like enough evidence to me!"

"Lying doesn't make you a killer. No, they need proof. Real, hard proof." She rubbed her arms.

"Are you too cold? The temperature's probably dropped fifteen degrees since earlier." I had to remind myself that Babe was in her seventies. Though she had the spirit of a teenager, her body was frailer than she let on.

"I'll be fine. The fresh air is good for me."

"Fresh air is nice."

"Didn't get much of this in Chicago, did you?"

I laughed, and found a new rock to abuse. "No, I will give Boring, Indiana, that. Everything just feels cleaner here."

Silence lagged, and the second rock somehow escaped me.

This would be the perfect time to tell Babe about the note. Out here, there were no listening ears. Even though I initially feared that Babe talked too much, I'd come to realize that I could trust Babe when it came down to important issues like this.

"I need to tell you something, Babe. But you have to promise not to tell anyone."

She gave me a quick glance before nodding. "Of course."

I checked behind me, just to make sure we were alone. The bright headlights of a souped-up golf cart glared at us from the distance. No doubt just some of the neighbors out being social. It wasn't unusual to see people cruising around the neighborhood in their golf carts. I assumed that was just something people in small towns did for fun.

I drew in a deep breath. "Somebody's threatening me, Babe."

I explained about the note.

Babe stopped in her tracks there on the sidewalk. "You haven't told Kent yet?"

I shook my head. "How can I? They said they'll kill him if I do."

"How will they know?"

"Because someone bugged my house!" Saying it out loud made me feel delusional.

"What are you talking about? Do you think we're a bunch of spies around here?"

"I'm serious. Someone bugged my house. They recorded a conversation between Kent and me and played it back to me over the phone."

"That's terrible. And invasive. You have to tell Kent." She grabbed my arm. "No wonder you feel distant from him lately, Laura. Secrets can divide couples."

Our troubles went deeper than that. We'd been divided before I got that letter.

Should I plunge deeper with Babe? Why not? I needed to get some things off my chest. "It's not only that, Babe. He's been going somewhere every Friday afternoon while at work. I found out by accident."

We began walking again. The golf cart still puttered behind us. I wished the driver would just go ahead and pass. Instead, he rambled on the sidewalk at a leisurely pace.

"Woman, you've got to ask him about it. No wonder you look so miserable."

My heart panged. "What if I don't like his answer?"

"What if it clears up this whole mess? What if there's a logical explanation, and you're fretting about it for no reason?"

"I don't want to face reality if that's not the case, though." It may be pathetic, but it was the truth.

"Laura, you've got to talk to him. For the sake of your marriage."

"I hate this, Babe. I hate what's happened to my marriage. Kent and I used to be so close, so in love. Now we're—we're just like friends."

"Marriage has its phases. Every marriage does."

"Even yours did?"

"Of course. You just have to remember the happy times. Dwell on those."

Kent and I did have happy times. Really happy times when I thought I might burst with the joy of finding my soul mate. What had time done to our relationship?

The golf cart was right behind us now, trolling along at a snail's pace. Its lights were so bright that I couldn't even see who was driving. I stepped onto the grass to let it pass. Babe followed my lead.

"You should tell the police about the note too. Maybe there's a fingerprint on it."

Babe was right. I should give the letter to the police. I wasn't sure why my stubbornness stopped me.

"Who in the world is driving that golf cart? Why doesn't it just pass us?" Babe turned and shielded her eyes from the blinding headlights.

The golf cart suddenly sped up. It was about time. I waited for it to zoom past. Instead, it veered from the sidewalk.

Right toward Babe and me.

# 17

"I guess this clears Jerry," I mumbled to Babe. Jerry had been at the police station handing over his financial information when the runaway golf cart came at us.

I rubbed my elbow, which was still sore from my tumble onto the grass. At least I didn't have tire marks across my skin. I'd come close—too close.

Babe and I sat across from Chief Romeo at the police station. We'd hobbled halfway back to my house after the golf cart sped away. Then Harry had pulled up and offered us a ride home. Kent had bandaged us and brought us straight here.

Right now, Kent waited in the lobby, pacing the last I'd seen him. Totally clueless about what had happened. I felt certain that Kent thought the incident was an accident, maybe someone with dementia who hadn't seen us walking. Kent wasn't the type to suspect foul play. He always thought the best about people.

I wished I could do the same.

Neither Babe nor I had gotten a good look at the driver of the golf cart. Its lights were too bright and, after unsuccessfully trying to run us over, it sped away so fast the person was just a blur.

Thankfully, neither of us was hurt.

"How do the two of you keep finding yourselves in the middle of this?"

"Good question." I nodded. "I have no idea."

"Maybe we're trouble magnets." Babe sounded a little too gleeful about that.

Chief Romeo sighed. "Well, I suggest you stay out of trouble. Whoever this killer is, he or she shouldn't be messed with."

I shifted in my seat. "Respectfully, sir, trouble always seems to find us, not the other way around."

"Is there anything else you two want to tell me?"

Babe looked at me and nodded. I sighed and spilled everything...well, almost everything.

"Candace was threatening to tell everyone that Donna has a criminal past. Donna is thinking about running against Hillary as president of the Homeowners' Association, and Donna thought the information would ruin her chances."

"Did Candace and Donna not get along?"

I looked at Babe. "You would know better than me."

"She, Tiara and Donna all used to be best friends. Only in the past month or so had they started to grow apart."

The chief leaned closer to me, his gaze intense. "Do you think Donna would kill Candace in order to save her reputation?"

"I suppose stranger things have happened." An invisible weight pressed on my chest, and I shrugged. "I'll leave you to find that answer, I guess."

The chief asked a few more questions before dismissing us with that same worn-out charge to contact him if we thought of anything else.

Kent greeted me with a hug when I stepped into the lobby. "You okay?"

I nodded. "I just want to go home."

※※※

I'd fallen asleep soon after getting home, maybe just to avoid talking to Kent or maybe out of exhaustion. I wasn't sure.

But the next morning, when Kent kissed me as he left for work, I felt instantly alert. I jerked myself to a sitting position in bed. When I saw Kent walking out of the bedroom door, I quickly grabbed my robe and threw it around me before following him.

"What about Candace's funeral?"

"I wish I could make it, but I don't have anyone to manage the pharmacy."

"Can't you miss just a few hours of work?" I stared at him in his suit and tie, looking very trim and handsome. And I wanted him with me. Not filling prescriptions. I needed him by my side.

"Laura, we knew this transition would be tough when we moved here. I can't afford to take time off. Not yet." He stepped closer and swiped a hair behind my ear. "You understand, don't you?"

I wanted to pout and whine and throw a little temper tantrum.

Instead, I said, "I hate going to funerals alone." Okay, it was still pouty and whiny but measured all the same.

"All your friends from the neighborhood will be there. You won't be alone."

Except they would all be with their husbands.

"I'll make it up to you, honey. We'll go out to dinner tonight, okay? We'll go wherever you want."

I raised my chin slightly. "Somewhere in the city?"

"Anywhere." He smiled and kissed me before glancing at his watch. "I've got to run. I'll see you tonight."

I nodded as he walked out the door. Tonight would be the perfect time to tell him about the note. We'd be out of the house, relaxed and alone. I made up my mind. Tonight was the night.

I stepped back and leaned against the wall, trying to clear my head. What happened to Mrs. Independent? I'd always prided myself on being strong and not needing a man while I was in college. Then I met Kent, fell in love, and realized how silly I'd been. Yet even in my marriage I'd fought to be strong, to make my own money, to not be too needy.

And now I was crumbling.

I shook off my self-pity and got dressed. Then I grabbed the casserole I'd prepared yesterday morning—a chicken cacciatore pasta bake. It looked pretty tasty, so hopefully the dish would be. I bundled up in a wool coat and threw my purse over my shoulder to leave.

Outside, the sun shone bright and the sky stretched blue and clear, yet a frosty wind zipped through the air. I braced myself and hurried down the sidewalk to my car.

A few minutes later, I pulled up at Boring Community Church.

I walked into the kitchen amidst a flurry of white hair. What was I supposed to do with this casserole? I'd never been asked before to cook something for a funeral, so this was a first for me.

"I didn't know you were bringing something, chickaroonie."

Thank goodness for Babe. She took the dish from my hands and ushered me to a table in the fellowship hall, which was bustling with activity.

"Where's Kent?" Babe called over her shoulder.

I fought a frown. "He had to work."

"Bummer. You mind if I sit with you instead? I promise not to play my Nintendo DS. That Brain Age game is really addicting. It keeps telling me I have the mind of an 18-year-old."

"I'd love the company." Good old Babe. Thank you, Lord. She's my saving grace. Well, You are. But Babe's Your angel.

"Just let me drop off your dish. It looks off the hook."

I smiled. "Totally."

She joined me a few minutes later, and we strode down the hallway toward the sanctuary. My gut churned, and I felt like I might vomit. Funerals had always had this effect on me, ever since I had to attend my grandmother's when I was 12. My hands trembled around the strap of my purse as we entered the sanctuary.

I still couldn't believe Candace was dead, murdered at that. Each morning, it seemed like I should wake up and discover the whole scenario to be merely a nightmare. Even with everything that had happened, Candace's untimely death still seemed like a B-grade horror movie.

I stared at the casket at the front of the room. Babe stepped toward it, but I stopped and shook my head. I never could deal with viewings at funerals. I held back and watched dear Babe, dressed in a black dress and wearing a hot pink scarf across her hair, peer into the coffin and shake her head, as if the death was a shame.

And it was a shame. I'd learned to stop questioning God about why some people's lives were snatched away early, before their time. I knew I'd never understand it. I understood that I'd never understand.

Babe came back and took my hand. She led me to a seat, midway in the sanctuary. As we sat, she patted my hand.

"Candace may not have been well-liked, but she didn't deserve this."

I glanced at Babe. "I couldn't agree more. The person who did this needs to be put behind bars."

"Very true, but this isn't the time to speak about it. This is the time to honor a friend."

I couldn't think of any better way to honor her than to find her killer, but I kept my thoughts to myself.

As the funeral began, I spotted Jerry on the front row. His face looked ashen, and his cheeks sunken. Being questioned for your wife's death could do that to a person.

I did know that the same person who killed Candace was

trying to kill me. And since Jerry was at the police station last night, he wasn't the one who tried to run me over. Maybe the man had no scruples, but he wasn't a killer.

Who did I know who owned a golf cart? It would be easier to narrow it down by listing everyone I knew who didn't own one. It seemed like almost everyone in the community had the things. Most of the men golfed on evenings and weekends. Even the preacher owned a cart.

I fought a sigh. I just couldn't stop trying to figure out who-done-it.

The preacher began the eulogy. I tried to listen, but my eyes scanned the full church. I spotted Donna and Tiara with their husbands on the other side of the room. They used tissues to dab their eyes. Could one of them have done it? Donna certainly had motive—a weak motive, but still a motive—and the evidence seemed to be stacking up against her. But—I came back to this time and time again—I couldn't see her killing someone. A few rows in front of me sat Harry, and a few rows in front of him was Chief Romeo.

Most of the town appeared to be here; the crowd even flowed into the foyer. Everyone—except Kent—seemed to want to pay their respects, even if Candace hadn't been well-liked. Babe told me that was just the way things worked in a small town.

Another thought hit me, causing goose bumps to sweep over my arms.

If most of the town was here, was the killer in this building right now?

❀❀❀

"You okay? You look like you've seen a ghost." Babe leaned toward me and offered me a Victoria's Secret breath mint. I politely refused.

"I just hate funerals," I whispered, as people filed out of the sanctuary.

"They're awful, aren't they? When I die, I want a celebration, not a cry fest."

I nodded. "You want people to celebrate your life. I like that."

"People don't need to cry for me. I'm going to be in a better place, a place where I can rollerblade without cracking any bones."

I smiled. "That sounds nice."

Heaven. What a comfort. To be able to sing with the angels, to meet the Creator on His own turf, to be reunited with loved ones.

But as wonderful as it sounded, I didn't feel ready to go there yet. My life felt unfinished.

Yet, if I wasn't careful, my arrival date into heaven just might come sooner than expected—if a certain killer had his way.

Most of the room had cleared, so Babe and I slid from the pew and followed the crowd back into the fellowship hall. I could already smell the savory scents of barbecue and fried chicken and other foods I couldn't quite identify. As my mouth watered, I momentarily felt guilty for forgetting about Candace.

"This is the best part of funerals," Babe whispered.

At least someone else shared my sentiments. The difference

was, I would never, ever voice the thought.

"I think I want a luau for my funeral. Maybe even leis, a roasted pig, lots of pineapple—slices on fruit trays, pineapple upside-down cake, grilled pineapple."

"Babe! A celebration is one thing, but a party is a totally different story. It would just seem irreverent to have a themed dinner after a funeral."

"I want a slideshow too, with lots of pictures from my life. You'll help with that, won't you, Laura?"

"Babe, I don't want to even think about that."

"Are you saying you'll miss me, chickaroonie?"

"Of course I'll miss you. You're my only friend." I blushed when the words left my lips. They sounded so pathetic.

"I'll miss you, too." She patted my shoulder. Her gaze locked on something across the room and suddenly she scowled. "What's he doing here?"

My shoulders tensed. "Who?" I followed her gaze and spotted the local bank owner. "Paul. Of course. Why do you dislike him so much?"

Her eyes narrowed. "There's nothing about him to like."

"He seems nice enough to me."

"Well, you don't know him like I do." She grabbed a plate and piled food onto it. "And count that as a blessing."

Another woman from church began chatting about the recipe for a congealed salad, so I couldn't question Babe any more. I still couldn't figure out the curious relationship between the two senior adults.

I shoved the thought to the back of my mind, and thought instead about where I wanted to go for dinner tonight.

"I hate funerals," Hillary whispered, spearing a cucumber slice as she came alongside me at the buffet.

I grabbed a ham biscuit. "Me too." I looked behind her. "Where's your husband?"

"Had to work. Yours?"

"Same."

Well, maybe Hillary and I did have something in common: We were both former career women with husbands who worked too much. Maybe Hillary wasn't that bad after all.

Something in her oversized purse caught my eye. I tried to look away but couldn't. *The Do-It-Yourselfer's Guide to Becoming a Private Eye*. Interesting.

Her hand went to her purse and her cheeks reddened. "You caught me."

"Thinking of starting a new career?"

A weak laugh escaped. "I'm just keeping tabs on Mark. I'm not the most trusting person. Please don't tell anyone, though. I know it sounds insecure."

"Your secret is safe with me."

"I've got to eat quickly and then get back home to work on the association's newsletter. The work never ends."

"You seem to enjoy it, though."

"I do. It's my life. That's why I have to put so much into my campaign. Have you thought anymore about helping?"

I grabbed a sausage ball. "I haven't made any decisions yet."

"Don't take too long, or you'll miss out."

And with that, she scurried away. She shook hands and mingled like a true politician.

I nibbled on my pimento cheese triangle and watched her. I wondered if she had an alibi for the day Candace died.

# 18

After the funeral, I wandered toward the pharmacy. Maybe I'd check on my husband, provided he was indeed working and not at a secret meeting again. Of course, today wasn't Friday, so I should be okay. I parked in the public lot and meandered toward my husband's dream—or lately, what felt like his mistress.

Maybe my problem was that I had too much time to think. Maybe I needed to put "the incident" behind me and look for another job. Of course, no one would want to hire me, especially with no references—and I'd never, ever put my former company down as a reference. Only if I wanted a death wish. Even if I started my own PR firm, my past would eventually catch up with me.

As I passed the bank, I remembered I had a deposit to make. Buying the pharmacy had sucked up most of our savings, and it could be awhile before we turned a profit. This check was the last of my severance package, and we needed to put it away for the mythical rainy day.

I stepped into the bank and spotted Paul sitting in his corner office. I bypassed the tellers and made a beeline toward him.

"Laura Berry! Good to see you. Just to let you know, I'm not dead. Yet." He grinned as he reached out to shake my hand.

My cheeks flushed as he pumped my arm up and down. "You're not going to let me live that down, are you?"

"What fun would that be?" As he sat, his smile turned more serious. "What brings you in today?"

"Just need to a make a deposit into my savings." I glanced at my check and shrugged. "And I thought I would say hi while I was at it."

"Your friend Ms. Pritchard isn't with you today?"

Now he had my attention. "No, she's cleaning up after the funeral."

"So sad to hear about Candace." He shook his head slowly. "What a shame. But the funeral was lovely."

"I know. And to think the killer is still out there."

He raised his eyebrows, and steepled his fingers in front of him. "God bless anyone who encounters him."

I shifted in my seat. "Or her."

He froze and stared at me. "Excuse me?"

"You said him. As if the killer is male." I leaned back in my chair. "The killer could very well be a she."

He smiled and shook his finger at me. "You're a smart one. I knew that from the first day I laid eyes on you."

My cheeks flushed again. "I haven't heard that in awhile, so thank you."

"You ever want to start working again, you come and see me."

"I'm afraid banks usually don't need PR reps."

"Well, this is no ordinary bank." He winked.

"I'll keep that in mind, Mr. Willis." I pushed my check forward. Just seeing the name of my old employer caused my gut to churn. "Now, if I could deposit this."

As he ran the check through a machine, I couldn't help but ask, "So, how long have you known Babe?"

He grinned that million-dollar-smile again. "What did she tell you?"

"Only that you used to own a jazz club."

He nodded as the machine squealed. "It's true. We go way back."

I waited for him to share more. Instead, he handed me a receipt. "It's always great seeing you, Mrs. Berry. Keep thinking about that job offer."

With no more answers than before, I moseyed to the pharmacy. As soon as I walked in, I glimpsed Kent in his white coat behind the pharmacy counter. He did look busy—and quite handsome, if I did say so. I also noticed his skin looked pale, as if he'd been inside too much. When we first started dating, we were constantly outside—having picnics, taking walks, searching for shooting stars. What was it about adulthood that kept us inside more? Full-time jobs, I supposed.

I couldn't believe our seventh anniversary was in less than a week. It was the one time of the year I knew Kent and I would take time for each other. Anniversaries were good for that. It was the one piece of hope I had for our relationship. When the rest of the outlook seemed bleak, romance was definite each year when we celebrated our wedding. Who cared that this year it fell on the same day as the Super Bowl?

Jasmine nearly collided with me as she rushed through the front door.

"Oh, Mrs. Berry. I'm so sorry." She grasped my arms to steady herself. Her eyes looked red, as if she'd been crying.

"It's Laura, and it's okay." I leaned closer when I felt her hands trembling. "Are you okay?"

She shook her head, and a tear escaped. "No, I'm terrible." She drew in a deep breath and sobbed. "I killed Candace Flynn!"

※※※

I stared at Jasmine as she sat in the booth across from me at the pharmacy, and I handed her a tissue. Her sobs had calmed down—slightly—but her confession had me more curious than a cat who'd discovered a mouse hole.

"Why would you think you killed Candace, sweetie?"

She sniffed, and her lips turned downward, a sure sign of the sob to come. Surprisingly, she pulled in a breath and blurted, "I promise, I didn't mean to. Everything's just been eating at me and now with the funeral—I felt so guilty."

"You said you didn't mean to. Didn't mean to what?"

She wiped her eyes with a crumbled tissue. "Provide the sleeping pills used to kill her."

I wanted to laugh, but I didn't. Instead, I patted her hand.

"You couldn't possibly have known. Your job is to simply fill prescriptions."

"That's exactly it. I didn't do my job. I let my emotions get in the way." The frown reappeared, followed by a wail. I saw Kent glance at us curiously. I shook my head, indicating for him to leave us be. He stared for another moment before turning back to the computer.

I leaned toward her, and lowered my voice. "Why don't you tell me what happened."

She wiped another tear. "I just always feel so bad when people don't have insurance. Prescriptions can sometimes be twenty or thirty dollars a pill."

"They can be expensive."

"Anyway, this one customer was practically in tears. Said she couldn't keep paying so much for her prescriptions, and her son's medications, and her husband's preexisting condition. It costs her almost four hundred dollars a month. That's a lot of money."

"What does this have to do with Candace?" I tried to keep my voice even, but inside, I wanted to scream, get on with it!

"I slipped a few extra pills into this woman's prescription. Every little bit can help, I figured. But I just know those were the pills used to kill Candace!"

I sucked in a breath. "Jasmine, who did you give them to?"

Tearful, her gaze met mine, and her chin trembled. "Donna Roberts."

Three hours later, Chief Romeo had picked up Donna for questioning. I guess the accumulation of evidence warranted her at least being brought down to the police station for further examination. The sleeping pills alone weren't enough to make her guilty—a lot of people in town took them, so why would an extra pill given by Jasmine have to be a part of the murder?

I imagined the scene taking place at the police station, and tension knit itself up and down my back like a too-tight polyester sweater.

After Jasmine and I had spoken, I'd insisted that we go together to the police station and share the news. That seemed more urgent than Jasmine telling Kent about her indiscretion. But now I had to face Kent and tell him the truth.

I dragged myself toward the front door. As soon as I stepped onto the stoop, Kent opened the door, his eyes on me. Why did I feel like I was the guilty one? Like he was accusing me of doing something wrong? Had I?

I silently walked past him and plopped on the couch. He sat across from me and I explained to him what had happened.

How could Jasmine have done this? She had come into town with no family and no work experience. Several families at church had taken her in. Kent had trained her to be a pharmacy technician, even paying her during in the process.

He rubbed his hands over his face. "This is bad, Laura."

"DEA bad?"

"They're probably going to question me as well. I'm the supervising pharmacist." He shook his head. "I trusted Jasmine. I can't believe she did this."

"I think her intentions were good." I didn't know whom I felt sorrier for: Jasmine or my husband. "She's naïve. This would have never come out except that Candace was murdered."

"Stealing is stealing, no matter which way you look at it." He ran his hands over his face again. "I don't think you realize how big a deal this is. There will be an investigation. I could lose my license."

"Lose your license?" Alarm shot through me. Kent loved his job. What would he do without it? We'd given up everything to come here. Our life couldn't go down the drain so quickly, could it?

I couldn't even bring myself to ask any questions. Living in ignorance beat reality at the moment. My thoughts shifted back to Jasmine. I don't know why she'd warmed my heart so quickly. But I just felt like the girl needed someone on her side.

"Will you fire Jasmine?"

"She'll probably lose her license."

"I feel bad for her. She doesn't have anyone to hold her up, to be in her corner. This has to be hard on her."

"Who'd she give the extra pills to?"

"Donna." Despite my optimism that the woman was innocent, I couldn't stay in denial forever.

"Donna?" He sat up straight. "Why Donna? I was expecting to hear the name of some poor, down-on-their-luck family. Not

Donna, who drives around in a Mercedes."

"Maybe things aren't always what they seem on the surface. Maybe they're having financial problems. It can happen to the best of us."

Sadness pressed in on me as the words left my mouth. Yes, problems could happen to the best of us.

# 19

The phone rang first thing Tuesday morning. After a long, fitful night filled with dreams about Jasmine and Donna, I awoke with a start. I grabbed the phone, fearing the worst: news about my husband being arrested, the pharmacy shutting down, and losing the boring life we'd given up everything to obtain.

Instead, I heard Babe's voice. "Donna is being held for Candace's murder."

I sat up in bed and ran a hand through my matted hair. "Really? Why?"

"You'll never believe this. You know those wipes Donna's always bragging about? The ones that clean anything, that you can only buy online?"

I remembered. Magic Wipes. Donna talked about them all the time. You'd think she had stock in the start-up company. "Yeah, I remember."

"That's what was used to smother Candace. The report

just came back today, I guess. They found trace evidence on Candace's face and mouth, and they found one of the wipes in the trashcan."

"No." I leaned against the headboard—a little too hard. I rubbed the back of my head.

"And her fingerprints were found on the remote that Candace was holding. I guess that, coupled with everything else, gave them enough to hold her. The chief has had a lot of pressure on him to make progress on this case and get the killer off the street."

With all of that pressure on him, had he made the right decision, though? I supposed Donna had means, motive, and opportunity, although none seemed strong enough to charge her.

"I expected a bigger reaction from you," Babe said. I could picture her tapping her foot impatiently.

I searched for the right thing to say. "I guess everyone can sleep better now." Bad choice of words considering the way we'd found Candace. "Everyone can *rest* better now. But what was her motive?"

"Don't know. I'm sure it will all come out soon, though. In the meantime, I'd watch your mailbox."

"My mailbox?" Was there an announcement about her motives coming to me soon or something?

"I saw her put something in there the other day."

I tensed. "What are you talking about?"

"I don't know. I didn't think anything of it at the time, but now that I know she's guilty, it made me think about what I saw.

I looked out my window and saw Donna put something in your mailbox. Now I'm thinking it's a good thing it wasn't a bomb or something."

"Babe—the note? The threatening letter I got?"

Her lips parted. "Oh, yeah. Oops."

My mind reeled. Donna was the one who'd left the banana bread—and the threatening note. Sometimes the answers were obvious. Donna must have assumed Kent knew about Jasmine giving her extra sleeping pills. She must have figured he'd put the puzzle pieces together eventually. But why hadn't she threatened Jasmine? Sure, Donna took sleeping pills. But so did a lot of other people in Boring.

Why couldn't Babe have told me that information... oh, I don't know...two weeks ago?

At least now I could eat in peace. I had to accept the fact that Donna had sent me that threatening letter. Somehow, she'd bugged my house and blown up my shed. Donna was guilty. Wasn't it always the innocent ones who ended up doing the crime? At least the woman was in jail now.

As soon as Babe and I hung up, the phone rang again. Hillary.

"The debate is cancelled tonight, but we still need to meet to discuss the future of this neighborhood. I'm calling everyone to let them know."

The debate. I'd nearly forgotten about the pre-election event between Hillary and Donna. "Okay. Thanks."

"One more thing. I need you to take over the treasurer position that Candace left vacant."

"Me?" I pointed to myself as if Hillary could see me.

"Only for a couple of weeks until the election. We need someone—other than me—in the position to keep things on the up and up."

"I don't know if I'm the right person—"

"I think so. Say you'll do it. Please. You're such a hard worker, I really think you're the best person for the job."

I shrugged. "Since you put it that way."

"Great. Let's meet to discuss a few things before tonight's meeting. It's really quite tragic about Donna, isn't it?"

"You heard too?"

"Everyone has. This is small town America. So, when can you come over? The sooner, the better."

My schedule today was the same as most days—nothing important penciled in—unless you included housework. "Just let me get dressed."

Thirty minutes later, I arrived at her house. Her husband's SUV waited in the drive. He must be taking the day off work.

As soon as I stepped inside, Hillary grabbed her purse and keys. "We've got to go to the bank so I can put your name on the paperwork." She walked out the door. "Come along."

I raised my eyebrows, but still swiveled to follow.

"It will only take a minute. Then I'll explain how everything works, and off you'll go. I'll announce you tonight."

"It seems like an awful lot of trouble for a two-week position."

"Rules are rules. We have to have a treasurer. Now that

Candace is buried and her killer is behind bars, I figured we could fill the position with a clear head."

Paul greeted us at the bank with his normal sparkle. I glanced down at his desk and noticed a Backstreet Boys CD with a name written in fingernail polish across it. Babe's!

What was Paul doing with it? Maybe Babe was right and he was nothing but trouble. In my mind, I saw his teasing in a different light—perhaps he was deranged, even stalking Babe.

My hackles went up.

"How are you today, Mrs. Berry?"

I nodded stiffly. "Fine."

He eyed me a moment, as if wondering about my aloofness. Hillary explained something about a fingerprint I'd need in order to balance the books or cut checks. As she spoke, Paul casually pushed the CD under a pile of papers. The action was so swift, I wouldn't have noticed had I not been watching the CD. He didn't miss a beat in the conversation.

I had to talk to Babe about this. I had to warn her.

What if the police had picked up the wrong killer? What if Donna didn't do it at all? What if that evidence had been planted? What if Paul was the real killer? He was the one with suspicious behavior around here.

After I was added to the account and Hillary and I were outside, I paused on the sidewalk. "I really need to stop by and see Kent. Can we talk about the treasury stuff tomorrow?"

Her gaze flickered, as if my choice didn't please her. Oh well.

"I suppose that will be fine."

I stuffed my hands deeper into my coat pockets. "Great. Thanks."

I bypassed her car and went into the pharmacy. Kent worked alone today, and I could see by the circles under his eyes that he was exhausted. His eyes brightened when I walked in.

"Hey, honey. What brings you here?"

I walked up to the counter and leaned toward him. "Did you hear?"

He continued to mark something on his clipboard. He glanced up in response. "About Donna? It's been all the talk today."

"Sad, isn't it?"

He nodded and paused from his work. "Incredibly. I would have never thought she could do something like that. I guess some people can really have you fooled."

Jasmine. He was talking about Jasmine and, based on his frown, he was truly disappointed to know his employee had stolen from him. "Any word about an investigation?"

Kent shook his head. "Chief Romeo sounds like he's willing to let this drop, if I am. He said there's no need to get the DEA involved in something this trivial. If Donna goes to trial and the stolen pill is presented as evidence, the issue might have to be revisited. Nothing's definite, yet, though. This could all still blow up."

I nodded, trying to look on the bright side. "And at least we can eat without fear again," I offered, figuring that news might cheer him up. Guys always cheered up when food was mentioned, right?

He stopped shuffling through papers, and his gaze fell heavily on mine. "What do you mean we can eat without fear?"

I shrugged. "You know, the poisoned banana bread and stuff."

He put the clipboard down and stepped closer. "You think Donna did that?"

I figured now was as good a time as any to tell him about the note. The threat didn't matter anymore—Donna was behind bars. My family was safe. "I didn't want to worry you, but I got this note right after Candace died, saying that you better keep your mouth shut or we'd both end up like Candace. Donna must have been afraid that Jasmine would spill the beans about that extra pills she doled out. It all makes sense now."

Kent's eyes were big and his lips tight. "Someone threatened us, and you didn't think it was important to tell me?"

I felt myself shrinking back. I thought he'd be relieved, to think of me as brave for protecting him with my silence. "The note said if I told anyone, we'd die."

His mouth gaped open, and he shook his head. "So you didn't tell me?"

"I didn't want you to die."

He leaned with his palms on the counter toward me. There was no amusement or gratefulness in his voice. Only disappointment. "I can't believe you kept that from me."

How could he be mad about this? Anger surged inside me. "I was trying to save your life!"

Kent opened his mouth as if to respond, then his gaze

flickered behind me. A customer approached the counter. He looked at me again and shook his head. "I have to get back to work."

"But—"

"We'll talk later, Laura." His voice sounded firm. He looked beyond me. "Can I help you, Mrs. Walker?"

The woman scooted past me and handed Kent a paper.

I didn't even have the chance to bring up rescheduling our missed date from last night. But that dinner was the least of my worries right now.

I felt like my world had crashed around me.

# 20

I felt even worse when I came home to my empty abode. My neighbor had killed another neighbor. My husband was mad at me for trying to protect him. And I just generally felt miserable about life.

And I couldn't stop believing that the wrong person had been arrested, that my husband didn't love me anymore, and that moving here had been one big, bad mistake.

Maybe I could rewind my life.

Wouldn't that be nice?

Instead, I cuddled on the couch with Mr. Sniggles—the Flynns' cat—in my arms. I guess with Jerry cleared I should return the feline sometime. I'd found comfort in having him waiting for me at home every day. He purred as I stroked his head.

I watched Rachael Ray reruns. Sure, I'd seen the recipes

before. Just a couple of weeks ago, my goal had been to become a different version of Rachael Ray, all perky and happy to be in the kitchen. I wanted to turn over a new leaf from career woman to housewife. I wanted to let go of the things that defined me and learn to be content simply as a child of God.

Was there anything I wasn't failing at?

I've had it, God. I'm hanging up my detective hat. I'm hanging up everything. What do You want me to do now? It's up to You. I'm tired of trying to do things on my own. I've just made a mess of everything.

I glanced at the calendar and saw the big day circled on Sunday. Surely Kent would put aside his anger in order to celebrate our anniversary, wouldn't he?

Besides, why did I feel guilty? Sure, I'd kept the note from him. But I'd done it to protect him. I had to get credit for that, didn't I? And what about his Friday afternoon outings? Was he forgetting about those and any other secrets he kept from me?

Marriage was definitely the hardest thing I'd ever had to do. It was work, pure and simple. Yet, it was also a delight—usually.

A car door slammed, and I peeked out the window. Maybe Kent had decided to come home early and apologize for being so nasty about my secret.

Only my car was parked in the driveway.

I glanced across the street and saw Harry walking up to the front door of my new neighbor's house. He glanced around him as he did so, as if checking for anyone watching. What was going on between the two men? I remembered their whispers while at the gym.

Maybe they had gone in together to kill Candace. Of course, I had no motive for either of them. Darius had said that Candace and Harry used to date. Steele and Gia were opening a futon store. But the dots still weren't connecting.

Besides, Donna was behind bars.

Of course, Jerry had been at the station being questioned before that. Maybe the Boring Police Department really didn't know what they were doing after all. Perhaps I wasn't being hypercritical in my analysis of them.

Harry disappeared inside the Brunos' house. I resigned myself to getting ready for the association meeting tonight. It started in an hour. How depressing was it that the only thing exciting about my evening was going to one of these meetings? I really did have to get a life.

By the time our meeting started, Kent was still working. He was probably happy for the opportunity to avoid me. I climbed in my car and drove to Boring High School, where Hillary would announce to everyone that I'd taken over the treasurer position. I still had no idea why she wanted me to fill the void, but nonetheless, the position was mine.

Hillary started the meeting by banging her gavel on the podium.

"Thank you, everyone, for coming to the meeting tonight. The good news is that we can all have a little more peace of mind since we know a killer is behind bars." She smiled. "In case you haven't heard, Donna Roberts is being held for the murder of

Candace Flynn. While I'm talking about Donna, this would be a good time to mention that, due to her current situation, our bylaws state she won't be able to run against me for president."

I looked around but didn't see Babe. It wasn't like my friend to miss a meeting—especially when it gave her the opportunity to make fun of Hillary and hear some good gossip.

"She's a rat," Karen Jones mumbled beside me.

"Who?"

"Hillary."

"Why do you say that?" I whispered.

"Harry saw her over at Candace's on the day she died. The police don't even want to touch her since her husband still owns half of the neighborhood."

Hillary was at Candace's on the day she died? Now that was news.

"But the police have Donna in custody."

"Donna is adamant that she didn't do it. She doesn't know how those cloths ended up in Candace's house."

"You've talked to her?"

"Shh!" someone behind us insisted.

Karen cast a dirty glance over her shoulder. "I stopped by this morning."

I hadn't realized that Karen and Donna were friends.

"And I'd now like to announce that Laura Berry has graciously agreed to step into the treasurer's position until it's time for our elections in two weeks. Laura is very experienced, and I feel she'll be great in this interim position." Hillary looked at me and smiled.

Why would Hillary have killed Candace?

"Laura, would you like to say a few words?"

My eyes widened. I hadn't been prepared to say anything, just to quietly fill the position and do the best I could with it until someone qualified took over the task. I couldn't refuse Hillary in a room full of people, though. I stood and smoothed out my slacks as I walked toward the podium.

I stared at everyone, images of the Chicago press conference flashing back to me. Of course, here, I wasn't surrounding by reporters hungry for hot gossip. Here, I was surrounded by neighbors hungry for hot gossip. I took a deep breath and tried to slow my racing heart.

"I'm honored that Hillary asked me to fill this position until someone else is elected. I just want to let everyone in Dullington Estates know that I'm here to serve the neighborhood. For the next two or three weeks, at least."

Everyone chuckled.

The rest of the meeting was routine. I counted down the minutes until it was over. All I could think about was Kent, and how upset he'd been with me. I hadn't kept the note from him to hurt him. I'd wanted to protect him. Why couldn't he see that?

Everyone filled the aisles to leave the meeting. Harry stood in front of me, chatting with Karen—whom I really wanted to speak with. I wanted more information about Hillary. Why was today the first I'd heard about her being at Candace's house? And was Chief Romeo really not investigating that tip? Did he need to, now that Donna had been taken into police custody? What if someone had set her up to take the fall? Everyone knew Donna was crazy about those cleaning wipes. Leaving one of them in the house would be a sure set-up. How could I find out if anyone else in the neighborhood used them? There had to be a way.

A piece of paper slipped from Harry's pocket. I reached down to grab it for him, in case it was important. My eye caught a glimpse of the words across the top first, though. Futon World. The Brunos' business.

I knew I shouldn't, but I slipped the paper into my coat pocket. I had a feeling this was one clue I wanted to see.

※※※

As soon as I got in my car, I pulled the paper from my pocket, and quickly scanned the text. It was a receipt. Harry had purchased a futon from the company. I guess there wasn't anything juicy about that.

I remembered Jerry telling me that Harry purchased a couch from him that he didn't like. He found another one in Indy that he liked better. Had he gotten that couch from Steele'? That would have been before the family moved here.

What was going on between the two men? That was one mystery I'd sure like to solve.

Someone suddenly banged on my window. I gasped and glanced through the glass.

Harry.

I tried to smile and act like I was okay. I didn't want to roll down the window, though. What if the man was a killer? What if he'd poisoned those pork rinds, intending to kill Jerry?

I waved at him. "How's it going?" I raised my voice so he could hear me.

He nodded and flipped his finger, trying to signal to put the window down. I carefully tucked the paper under my leg so he wouldn't see it and then raised my hands into a "whoops" position.

"It's broken," I shouted.

He scrunched his eyebrows together then shrugged. "You all set for neighborhood watch tonight?"

I'd almost forgotten. "I'm ready."

"You and Babe give me a call if you have any trouble, okay?"

"Got it."

"And get that car window fixed soon. You never know when you might need to escape through it."

I stared at him.

"Sorry, I just watched a Dateline special about a car that went off a bridge."

I nodded. Maybe that made sense. I just hoped that Harry wasn't getting any ideas about how to off me if I figured out he was guilty.

※※※

I had just enough time between when I got home and when I started my Neighborhood Watch shift to visit the website for

Magic Wipes. Apparently, the wipes were organic and contained no chemicals.

With a little searching, I found the contact information for a representative who sold them in Indiana. The woman lived about an hour from Boring, close enough that she would be the logical sales contact for anyone buying the product in our town.

I punched in her number. A moment later, a perky voice came over the line. "This is Sally, a Magic Wipes representative. Magic Wipes can magically wipe away your worries about dirt and harmful chemicals. How can I help you?"

"I'm interested in ordering your product. I've heard good things about it."

"Wonderful!" Her voice went even more high-pitched than earlier. "How many would you like?"

"How about four boxes to start with?"

"Excellent. I assure you, you won't be disappointed. I'm just in love with this product. I can't stop talking about it! In fact, I don't have to work—my husband makes plenty of money. But I believe in this product so much that I decided to forget about the easy life and follow my passion!"

"That's...great."

"Now, let me get your information."

"I was hoping I could combine shipping with one of my neighbors. I like to save money wherever I can."

"Who is your neighbor, sweetie?"

"A couple of them use it. Do you have any shipments going to Boring, Indiana, any time soon? For a Donna Roberts? She said she orders from you."

"Oh, Donna in Boring! I just love Donna from Boring! Let me check my records here." I heard typing in the background. "I'm trying to talk her into become a Magic Wipe rep also. She'd just be perfect. But she doesn't have any orders for this month."

"It seems like I know someone else here who uses them, I just can't remember who exactly."

"I'm not supposed to do this—confidentiality and all—but let me see if there's anyone else. Oh, here you go. Tiara Swain has an order that's going out on Monday. Is that early enough?"

"Tiara uses Magic Wipes?" My adrenaline surged.

"Of course! She was one of my first customers, before Donna even. She orders every month. You will, too, once you try them."

I tapped my pen against my chin. "Good to know. Very good to know."

# 21

Neighborhood Watch time. Again.

Patrolling the 'burbs wasn't nearly as exciting as I'd thought.

Babe and I cruised the neighborhood, wearing our official shirts, of course. My thoughts skittered from Harry to Tiara to Donna to Hillary. There didn't seem to be a shortage of suspects who could have killed Candace.

"You're quiet," Babe said.

"Just thinking."

"About what?"

"About the meeting tonight. Where were you, by the way?"

"I had a previously scheduled engagement."

I raised an eyebrow. "Really. You have a hot date you're not telling me about?"

She snorted. "You're crazy. Now, tell me about the meeting tonight. How was it?"

I gave her a brief rundown.

We ran out of things to talk about after that, and I simply let Babe sing along with Beatles songs over and over.

How did Harry do this every night? I would lose my mind. Street after street of the same thing: nothing. People in this neighborhood went to bed early. There weren't even any cars driving around.

Boring lived up to its name, proudly.

"Why aren't you working anymore, Laura?"

My head swung toward her in shock. "What?"

"Working? You know, what you used to do for a living to make money. Why haven't you looked for a job here?"

I cleared my throat. "That's out of the blue, isn't it?"

"I've been wondering for awhile. A lot of people have. I mean, you seem like a career woman. You look pretty miserable as a housewife, to be honest."

"I'm not ... miserable. Not really." I didn't sound convincing, not even to myself.

"So, why aren't you looking for a job up in Indy or something?"

"It's a long story."

"We've got all night."

Suddenly, I felt trapped by the car. I had no way to avoid telling Babe the whole embarrassing story—unless I saw a suspicious activity.

I pointed in the distance. "Was that someone moving over there?"

"It was a tree branch. You're avoiding my question."

My shoulders sagged. Why put off the inevitable? I had to start talking about the whole fiasco eventually. "There was this little incident at the firm where I worked."

"Incident? Keep going." She rolled her hand in the air, as if telling me to speed it along.

I sighed. "I worked in public relations. I was about to be named a junior partner."

"Oh, this is going to be good!"

"Babe! This is my life, not a made-for-TV movie."

The sparkle disappeared from her eyes. "Of course, chickaroonie. I'm sorry for sounding insensitive."

"One of our clients had this catastrophe of sorts—she was admitted into a mental hospital. We held a press conference, trying to clear the air and do damage control."

"Why is that a catastrophe?"

"Because the person is famous, a celebrity. The press was all over it, especially since this person had gone on record as saying she didn't believe in medicating those with mental illnesses."

"What happened?"

The whole incident flashed back in my head, and I wanted to clench my eyes closed. "The CEO of the company issued the talking points for our press release, and sent me out to present them. I questioned a few of the points. I thought he offered too many details about what happened. I thought it would embarrass our client."

"And?"

"He insisted that this person's manager had okayed it, and

basically he pushed me in front of a bunch of reporters. I stuck to the script. Later, the celebrity sued us for making that information public. She said her manager didn't have the authority to release the information."

Babe grimaced. "Oh."

I nodded. "Yeah, oh no. Let's just say that someone had to take the fall for it. And since I was the one in front of the microphone—"

"That's terrible."

"What's worse is that my humiliation occurred in front of everyone in the public relations industry. There's no one who will hire me after that. I'm a laughingstock." My cheeks felt warm at the mere thought.

"You just followed your boss's orders."

"I should have trusted my gut. It turned out the celebrity's manager was just trying to keep her client's name in the headlines. We played right into it. I just felt awful."

"What did you learn from it?"

Again, my head swung toward her. "Excuse me?"

"Bad things happen in life, no matter who you are. You've got to take those lemons and make lemonade."

"What possible good thing am I supposed to take from being publicly humiliated?"

"You moved here, didn't you?"

"Oh, and that's been such a great thing." I rolled my eyes. "I've been bored out of my mind, and the only fun thing I can do is try to find a killer, which it turns out I'm terrible at. I don't know what I'm worse at—public relations or solving murders."

Babe scowled. "Your move here hasn't been all terrible, has it?"

"I can't think of one single good thing that's come from it!"

As soon as the words left my mouth, I realized what I'd said. "Oh, Babe. I didn't mean that. Of course I love my friendship with you. I'm sorry I said that."

She raised her chin, and I could tell I'd hurt her. "Boring is the best little town I've ever lived in. The people are good. They're hard workers. Maybe they're too simple for your tastes, but I think the people here are topnotch!"

Shame filled me. "They are topnotch. I'm sorry."

"You're too busy feeling sorry for yourself to see it."

"I don't feel sorry for myself." Did I?

"Could have fooled me. All I ever hear about is how awful your life is, how miserable Boring is, how terrible your marriage has become. When are you going to take responsibility?"

I pressed my lips together and silently drove for a few minutes. What did Babe know about my life? Nothing. "You don't understand."

"I understand that sometimes life takes you in a different direction than you'd planned, and you can either pout about it or make the best of it."

I wanted nothing more than to drop Babe off at her house and never speak to her again. Except I really didn't want to do that. I loved Babe.

She turned the radio up, and we cruised the neighborhood,

devoid of conversation for the next two hours. Nothing was happening in Boring, but I couldn't mention that to Babe or she might think I was whining. I didn't even know why we were doing Neighborhood Watch Patrol anymore since Donna was behind bars.

Lights in the distance caught my eye. Yes, there was life in Boring. At least one person had ventured out late into the night, a near sin for this town.

I was in a bad mood, with nothing but my thoughts to turn over and over. Thoughts about Babe's ill-hearted comments, about lemonade and being sour.

"Where's that car going?" Babe asked, all inflection gone from her voice.

I watched it a moment before turning off my headlights. "It's pulling onto our street. I think it's that new family."

"Cut the engine, too."

"Why?"

"Just do it."

I didn't feel like arguing with Babe anymore, so I did what she said. We sat in the car in dark silence. I watched as Steele and Gia pulled into their driveway. No one got out from the car, though. I wondered why.

Babe turned off the dome light, opened her car door and slid a leg out.

"Where are you going?"

"I'm getting out," she snarked.

"I can see that. Why?"

"Because whoever is in that car is staying in their car. They're probably afraid we're going to see them."

"I think you're reading too much into this."

"Am I?"

"Babe."

"Come on. What do we have to lose?"

Absolutely nothing except some boredom.

We quietly slipped from the car and then dodged behind the houses until we had better view of the Brunos. Gia and Steele slipped out of their black SUV. They wore all black, and looked around as if afraid someone was watching them.

Babe and I looked at each other. What was going on? They sure didn't look innocent.

We took the long way to the Brunos' backyard—first skirting the lake behind Babe's house, my house, and then Tiara's. Finally, we hid behind the Bruno's shed. From our vantage point, I could see right into their living room.

My eyes widened when I saw them pull out something from their duffle bag.

Spray paint.

Now, just what were they doing with that?

"We better get back to our car."

We sprinted back to the SUV just in time for Chief Romeo to pull up.

"Ladies." He nodded. "Are you on duty tonight?"

"We sure are," I responded.

"Tiara called and said she saw someone creeping around

behind her house. Know anything about that? Have you seen anyone suspicious?"

Yeah. Us. I kept my mouth shut.

"It's been as boring as ever around here tonight," Babe said. "We're just looking for some excitement."

"No, boring is good." I remembered Karen's accusation tonight at the association meeting. This would be the perfect time to ask the chief if he'd heard anything about Hillary.

"Have you questioned Hillary yet?" I blurted.

The chief looked startled at my question. "Excuse me?"

"I heard someone saw her at Candace's house on the day she died."

"As a matter of fact, we heard that same rumor and questioned her. It turns out she has an alibi. Several of them, to be exact. She was at a banquet up in Indy. Several people remembered seeing her there."

For some reason, the news disappointed me.

I got back in the car and cruised. Nothing happened for the rest of the night.

I got home in time to crawl in bed and sleep until the phone woke me up.

It was Chief Romeo.

"Laura, someone ransacked the pharmacy. You and Kent better get down here."

# 22

The pharmacy looked like a person who'd been beaten in a brawl.

The front windows had been smashed. Graffiti—boasting messages like "Go Away, City Slickers!"—slashed across the remaining walls. Shelves had been ransacked. Medications were missing. How would we ever recover from this?

I thought I saw tears in Kent's eyes. This store was his baby. And now someone had ruined everything.

We stood with our arms around each other, staring at the storefront like two people who couldn't tear their eyes away from tragedy.

Chief Romeo approached, doing his normal shirt-tuck. "Any idea who might have done this?"

Kent shook his head. "I have no idea. As far as I know, I haven't made any enemies since I moved here. I'd like to think I've made a lot of friends."

I remembered the Brunos coming home in the middle of the night, and cleared my throat. "I saw the Brunos with spray paint last night. They got in late, maybe late enough to have done this first."

Chief Romeo took notes as I told him what I'd seen. "We'll talk to them. In the meantime, I think you should call your insurance company. I'll get a couple of guys to board up the windows for you until we get things figured out."

I cleared my throat again. "Chief Romeo, just out of curiosity, who discovered the vandalism?"

"Harry called early this morning to let us know he'd driven past and seen it."

Harry. His name sure had come up a lot lately.

I nodded and mumbled "thank you" as he walked back toward the remains of the pharmacy.

Kent and I remained at the building, staring at the destruction. Several townspeople wandered past and offered condolences.

"I'm sorry this happened." Paul from the bank approached us. "You reckon it was someone trying to get drugs? I hate to think of people in Boring as being addicts, but I guess you can't get away from crime like that, no matter where you go."

"Drugs would be the obvious reason," I said, "but why paint these messages? Why say such awful things?"

"People are strange. It's hard to say why they do what they do." Paul patted Kent's shoulder. "Let me know what I can do to help you."

The rest of the day was a blur of talking to our insurance man, filling out paperwork, and waiting for the store to be released by the forensic team so we could get inside.

A question haunted me: Was this vandalism in any way related to my snooping into Candace's murder? I mean, why the pharmacy, of all places in town? There had to be a connection.

Finally, Romeo told us to go home and get some rest, that he'd call us when he knew something. Apparently the Brunos had an alibi—they were at a club in Indy where people spray-painted the walls. More than ten people could attest to seeing them there.

Which left us at square one.

Kent looked totally dejected in his recliner. He didn't even turn on the TV.

I knelt beside him and tried to find the right words. "It can be fixed. Everything that someone did last night to the pharmacy can be mended."

"Maybe." Kent stared at the wall.

I took his hand. "I'm sorry, honey. I know you love the store, and money's been so tight, but we'll get through this. Things always have a way of working out."

"Maybe this is a sign."

I tensed. "What's a sign?"

"The pharmacy and what happened to it. The threats on your life. On my life. Everything. Maybe this is a sign that we shouldn't be here." He finally looked at me. The loss I saw in his eyes saddened me.

I shook my head slightly, sure I hadn't heard him correctly.

"What?"

"You're miserable here, Laura. I know you are. You try to hide it, but you can't. You miss Chicago and our old life." Kent stood and shook his head. "Maybe this was all a bad idea. I was chasing a crazy dream, and I pulled you into a mess in the process."

"What are you saying?"

"Let's go back to Chicago."

I blinked. I couldn't believe he was saying this, the words I'd longed to hear since we moved to this place. I could go back to my friends, I could find a new job, I could wear cute shoes.

But my husband would be miserable.

"Kent, this is your dream. You can't give up on it." The lights of Chicago faded from my happy place.

"I think this was all a mistake. I'm sorry, Laura." His shoulders heaved with a sigh. "I mean, I'm working too much anyway."

I'd never seen Kent like this. But my own dreams began getting in the way of his. This was my chance to leave this place with all of its yawns and snores. Why would I encourage him to stay?

Sure, it would be a pain to move again, but the trouble would be worth it. We were both city slickers at heart. Living in Chicago didn't make us bad people.

"I'll talk to someone about selling the business tomorrow." He kissed my forehead, all light gone from his eyes. "Now, if you don't mind, I could use some time alone."

"Sure." I turned to walk away, to give him space.

"And Laura?"

"Yes?"

"I'm glad you're okay. That's the important thing."

"That I'm okay?"

"With everything going on lately, I'd rather they target the store than you."

I tilted my head. "Really?"

"Of course really." He cupped my face with his hand. "I'm going to go stare at the TV for a little while."

I nodded. "I'll take a walk."

I started walking and couldn't stop. Before I knew where I was heading, I'd left the neighborhood, passed the school, and stood at the edge of downtown Boring. I just couldn't seem to stay away from the store. I wanted to see it again, even though I knew it still looked the same as it did earlier.

My cell phone rang as I stood across the street from the building. I pulled it from my purse and answered.

"Laura? It's Megan Staples. How are you?"

Megan was one of the partners with the publicity firm where I'd worked. The last person I expected to call. I hadn't talked to her since "the incident."

"Megan! Wow. I'm okay. And you?"

"Listen, I have a question for you. I've left the firm."

"Really? I didn't ever see that happening." Like never, ever.

"I didn't like what they did to you. I'm starting my own company, and I'd like for you to come work for me."

My heart skipped a beat. "Are you serious?"

"Dead."

Dreams of being back in PR work flooded my mind. Being in the hustle and bustle of things, dressing up, meeting clients, feeling important. "Wow, Megan, that would be great."

"So you'll do it?"

I glanced at the pharmacy. I remembered the conversation I just had with Kent. Would we really move from here? And why did I feel a little sad at the thought?

"I need to talk to my husband, but I think he'd be open to moving."

"Okay, do that and get back with me. I really think we could start something big and go a long way with it. I know that whole debacle before you left wasn't your fault."

I hung up and felt in awe. Was this God's way of working everything out? Were we supposed to move to Boring as a test of faith and now somehow we'd passed and were able to return to our real life? Maybe I could feel some sense of purpose again, other than trying in vain to track down a killer.

For the first time in months, excitement surged through me. Maybe I could finally leave this place behind. Even the cool stillness of the day couldn't move me from my spot in front of the pharmacy. Maybe Kent was right. Maybe this was some kind of sign.

As I made my plans for the move back to Chicago, I thought I saw movement inside the pharmacy. I stepped closer. The police had all left. Crime scene tape still prevented people from entering the building—including Kent and me. Perhaps a bird had gotten inside? Was that what the movement was?

I squinted my eyes, hoping to get a better look. A flash of blue swept by the window. Someone was definitely inside. And I knew who.

※※※

"Harry! What are you doing in here?"

I took my phone out and dialed the police station. I wasn't going to confront a killer like some stupid chick from a horror flick. I didn't have a gun with me, but I had the power of communication. One wrong move, and I'd hit "send".

Harry stuck his head out the door, his hands in the air. "This isn't what it looks like."

"Then you'd better start explaining." I left my finger on the "send" button and pointed the phone at Harry like a weapon.

"I was just looking for evidence." He stepped from the store, hands still in the air. He looked to the left and right, probably seeing if anyone was witness to his humiliation.

"What kind of evidence?" Evidence that he'd been the one to vandalize the building, maybe? I continued to point the phone at him.

"I'm trying to figure out who did this."

"Why don't you just admit that it was you? You did it, Harry. And you killed Candace. You intended to kill Jerry, but Candace ate those pork rinds."

He shook his head with strong, swift movements. "I would

have never killed Candace. She was my first love."

"And you never forgave Jerry for stealing her from you." I could guess with the best of them. Now we'd see if I was right.

"It wasn't like that. I'm trying to figure out who killed her. I want to solve this case more than you do."

"So, why are snooping around on the other side of a police line?"

He stepped closer and I held up my phone, threatening to push the button. He backed off. "I have to figure out who did this. It's my only chance of ever making the police force. If I can solve this murder, people will take me seriously. Maybe I can quit being the cable guy for a living."

"You really expect me to believe that."

"It's true."

"I think you and Steele Bruno plotted all of this together."

"Bruno?" He snorted. "Why would you think that?"

"Because I've seen you whispering. I know about what happened between you and Jerry when he sold you that couch. You were mad. And what better way to get even with him than by going in with his competition to put him out of business."

"It's not like that."

"Why should I believe you?"

"Because, it's not true. Sure, I was mad at Jerry. He was a jerk. He's been a jerk to a lot of people around here. He's sold couches that are scratched, lumpy and have springs that stick you every time you sit down. But I didn't kill his wife."

I shook my head. "I'm not convinced."

"I may be a hothead and a cheapskate, but I'm no killer."

"You can put your hands down. I promise not to zap you with my phone."

He lowered his arms and chuckled. "You're tougher than I thought you'd be."

"Someone destroyed my husband's dreams. I take that seriously."

"Then you might want to know what I found in there. Evidence that the police missed." He reached into his pocket.

I stepped closer. "What?"

He held out his hand. It was a pen from Boring National Bank.

# 23

The pen could have been left there by someone who'd come in to sign for a prescription. The pen itself didn't implicate Paul Willis.

Of course, Paul Willis was already on my short list. I didn't like the tension between him and Babe. After I'd seen her CD on his desk, he moved up a few spaces.

Babe. I wondered if she was still mad. I wondered how she would react when I told her we'd probably be moving back to Chicago.

I really did appreciate her friendship. I knew I'd miss her more than anything if we moved.

I shuffled down the street. I needed to swing by the bank before it closed. I wanted to get a printout of all the transactions for the association. Hillary hadn't told me to do it, but I just wanted to take care of all the details. Thankfully, I'd only agreed to take the position for a couple of weeks. I'd get things in order in time for Kent and me to move.

I needed to start thinking about a real estate agent and where we'd live back in Chicago. I wondered if Kent could get his old job back.

"Can I help you?" the teller asked. I glanced over my shoulder and saw Paul at his desk. Today, I would avoid him. No need to interact with a possible killer.

What if that pen had dropped out of his pocket while he was vandalizing the store? Maybe he knew I was suspicious of him and he wanted to get me out of town.

Wait. If someone wanted to force me out of town, and now I was moving, then I was letting them win.

I'd have to think about that later.

I explained to the teller what I needed. She listened and took my fingerprint and then hurried over toward Paul. I inwardly groaned when I saw him heading my way.

"Mrs. Berry! Didn't expect to see you in here. How are you holding up? Have they caught whoever did that to the pharmacy?"

"Not that I know of. I'm sure the police are closing in on the person, though."

Paul winked. "You must have a higher respect for our police force than I do, then."

"I'm sure they're quite capable."

Paul leaned on the counter toward me. "So, you want a statement with your account balance on it?"

"And the transactions. I only have the ledger that Candace

kept. I'd like to have something to compare it to."

"Sounds wise." He straightened his papers. "We'll get that for you." He started to walk away. "Thanks for your business, Mrs. Berry. It's always good to see you."

Could that man really be a killer?

You know what? I didn't have to think about it anymore. We could get out of town and leave this whole mess behind us.

That sounded like the best plan so far.

A few minutes later, the teller appeared with my statement. I tucked it into my purse and began walking back home. I wondered how Kent was doing. Hopefully he wasn't too miserable. Maybe he was also finding comfort in the thought of moving away from this place. I hoped he'd eventually see the bright side.

When I got home, Kent was sleeping. I tiptoed from the room and went into our office. There, I pulled out the ledger that Hillary had given me, the one Candace kept.

I made copies of both of them, and then placed the copies side by side. I'd check off things as they matched up, just to make sure everything was balanced as it should be.

Forty minutes later, I was going cross-eyed. None of the numbers made sense. There were extra withdrawals for which I had no records. No wonder Candace's business was about to go bust. If this is the way she kept books, she was lucky the store had stayed afloat as long as it did.

What if Candace was stealing money from the association? She was in the perfect position to do just that. What if someone had found out and killed her for it?

My mind reeled. I couldn't help but think I was on to something.

The doorbell rang, and I hurried to answer it before the sound woke up Kent. Tiara was on the other side. Tiara, who had also ordered a case of Magic Wipes. Was there anyone who wasn't a suspect in my mind?

Not really. It seemed everyone either had motive or opportunity. What I needed was someone who had both.

But I wasn't going to mess with the investigation anymore, I reminded myself. I had other things to think about, things like tying up the loose ends of this new treasurer position and moving.

"I just heard what happened. How are you doing?" Tiara asked. It didn't seem right to see her at my door without Donna. In fact, I hadn't really talked to her since Donna had been accused of Candace's murder.

"I'm doing okay. Thanks for asking. Would you like to come in?"

She settled on the couch. "I just don't know what's wrong with this town. I mean, it's usually so peaceful. Here lately, it just seems like everything is so messed up."

I bit my lip. "How's Donna? Have you talked to her?"

"I visited her yesterday. She's doing about as well as can be expected." Tiara leaned closer. "She didn't do it, Laura. I know her. She's not capable of it."

"Do you think someone set her up?"

Tiara wiped away a tear. "It's the only thing that makes

sense. I think she's being framed and I'm afraid she's going to end up taking the fall for this. I just feel so badly for her family. I mean, blended families aren't easy anyway, but then to have all of this thrown on you—"

"I'm sure the police will figure things out." I patted her hand.

"And now your store. Why would someone do that? I just don't understand."

I shrugged. "I don't know either. Someone thinks I know something about Candace. They're trying to keep me quiet."

"Well, it obviously can't be Donna, can it? She was behind bars when the pharmacy was ransacked."

"That's true." Why was the killer still trying to silence me, even when someone else was charged with the crime? What sense did that make? And how did Candace's position as treasurer of the association tie in with all of this?

Would I ever know the answers?

❧❧❧

The numbers stayed on my mind into the evening. Kent had finally awakened, but insisted on drinking hot tea and watching TV for awhile. At least that had returned to normal. He definitely wasn't in the mood to chat.

I called Chief Romeo for any updates; he said they didn't have any. They had taken fingerprints, and were questioning several people who may have seen something. He promised to call if they found out anything.

"Kent, I'm going to run over to the Flynns' for a minute.

I need to see if Candace has any more books she kept for the association."

He mumbled, "Okay." Before I left, I spotted Mr. Sniggles and decided to see if Jerry was ready to have his pet back yet. I gathered the kitty in my arms, and hurried across the street.

"I'm sorry, Mr. Sniggles. I'd let you stay here if I could, but you're not mine." I nuzzled him a moment before knocking on Jerry's door.

When he answered, I knew he'd been drinking. I could tell by the smell, and by the slur of his words.

"Hi Jerry. How are you?"

He didn't answer. He didn't need to. "What do you want?"

I held up the cat. "I thought you might want your cat back."

He shrugged. "Not really. He was Candy's."

"Maybe he'll cheer you up."

"Nothing can cheer me up. I filed bankruptcy today."

"I'm sorry, Jerry."

"They're foreclosing on my home."

My heart panged in grief for him. "What can I do for you?"

"Yvonne even dumped me."

The poor guy had it rough. "Can I call someone for you?"

"There's no one to call."

"Jerry, let me fix you a cup of coffee." Coffee always seemed to help. Besides, I didn't know what else I could do.

He opened the door and allowed me inside.

The place looked a mess, much worst than it had even when Babe and I discovered Candace. Minus the dead body, of course.

I rummaged around in his kitchen until I found the coffee and filters. Then I started a pot. He dropped onto the couch and stared vacantly at the TV. I didn't know what to say. I remembered a friend of mine who was now a counselor about an hour from here. Maybe Jerry would talk to her.

I set a mug of coffee on the end table, hoping he'd drink a little and sober up. "Can I write down the number of someone who can help you? She's really great. I think you'd like talking to her."

"There's paper on my desk." He pointed his head into the front room.

I could tell he really didn't care, but I'd write down her number anyway. I went into the formal living room, which doubled as an office. Piles of paper tottered everywhere. I shoved a few aside on his desk and found a notepad.

Candace's planner sat in the corner. I heard Jerry mumbling at the TV in the other room. I ignored my conscience and opened the book. I scanned the week before she had died, hoping for a clue.

She had a lot of store meetings written down, but little else.

But there, on the day before we found her, was a small notation.

I squinted to read it. Meet with Paul Willis.

Funny, Paul never mentioned that. I wondered what they had to meet about. Could it be significant to her demise?

I quickly jotted down my friend's phone number for Jerry and ripped the paper from the pad.

"Here's my friend's number. Call her. You've got to pull yourself together, Jerry. Throw away your alcohol." I placed the paper on the coffee table.

He nodded and took a sip of his drink.

I slipped outside and returned to my own problems at home.

※※※

"I called my old boss back in Chicago." Kent sat up on the couch as I walked into the house. "He said my old position is still available if I want it. The person they hired after I left didn't work out."

I sat down beside him. "It's funny you say that, because out of the blue Megan called today, and she's starting her own PR firm. She wants to get me on board."

"Maybe moving here was a mistake."

"Maybe we were supposed to learn something."

"Have we learned it?"

I shrugged. "I suppose we have. I mean, look how everything is falling into place. It's like we're supposed to leave. Maybe we won't know the reason we were brought here anytime soon. But eventually it will all make sense."

"Yeah, I guess this was all just a crazy dream. I'm sorry I pulled you into it."

"You didn't pull me into it. I came willingly."

"And I love you for trying." He kissed my forehead.

Everything would be all right. I felt it, deep in my gut.

"Kent, about that note—"

"Let's just put all of that behind us. Donna is behind bars, and we have to look toward the future. Okay?"

I nodded and cuddled up in his arms.

# 24

Kent and I needed to go to the pharmacy the next day, but first, I slipped out to do a couple of errands. I had loose ends to tie up in anticipation of moving. One of those loose ends was talking to Donna—or, being neighborly, as Babe would say. An officer escorted me to her cell. Seeing her behind bars shook me up. Normally, Donna was so put together. Here, she had no make up. Her hair looked limp and greasy. She wasn't smiling.

She stood when she saw me. "Laura. What are you doing here?"

"I wanted to check on you." I approached the bars, knowing I had to find out why she'd targeted me and bugged my house. I just couldn't make sense of it. "How are you?"

She shrugged, her chin trembled, and she burst into tears. "I've been better."

"Do you want to talk about it?" Now why did I have to go and ask her that? She'd threatened to kill me!

"I don't know what there is to say. My life is falling apart. My stepkids hate me. My real kids hate my stepkids. I never see my husband because he works an hour and a half away, so I'm always the one who's trying to referee. Plus, there's this whole issue of being held in jail for a crime I didn't commit and my prior criminal record being paraded in front of anyone who's interested."

"I'm so sorry." And, for a moment, I was sorry.

"Did you hear about the whole criminal history thing?" Donna wiped her eyes again.

I hated to be honest, but I had to. "I did hear something. But I don't know any of the details, if that makes it any better."

"It was Candace's fault that word got out about it." She turned a sharp gaze on me. "But I didn't kill her."

"I didn't say you did."

She ran a hand over her face. "Candace didn't want me to run for president."

"Any idea why?"

"She said Hillary was doing a great job, which was ironic, because usually she talked about how much she hated Hillary. Still, she was determined I wouldn't dethrone the queen."

I shifted the weight on my feet. "Do you mind if I asked what happened?"

"I went to jail for a few months on battery charges when I was in my early twenties. I got into a fight with my boyfriend's ex. It wasn't pretty, and I regretted it. I was charged with a Class B Misdemeanor."

"I can't imagine what going to jail for that long would be like." I really couldn't.

"I wouldn't wish it on anyone."

My heart twisted for her. I really didn't think this woman was a killer. But there was something I had to ask her. "Donna, why'd you send me that threatening letter?"

She blinked. "Letter?"

"The one you put in my mailbox? Babe saw you."

"I didn't put anything in your mailbox. I don't know what you're talking about."

I resisted the urge to tap my foot. "Babe saw you, Donna. There's no need to deny it."

"The only thing I ever put in your mailbox was an envelope addressed to you that was accidentally put in my mailbox."

I blinked this time. "You mean, that's why you put the letter in there?"

Her mouth sagged open. "You thought I'd threatened you?"

"That's what seemed to make sense at the time."

"I would never do that, Laura. Never."

I believed her. I don't know for certain why I believed her—it was mostly a gut feeling.

And if she told the truth, that meant there was still a killer out there. The thought pressed heavily on me. "I guess I should have asked you about it earlier. I'm sorry, Donna. You always seem like you have it all together. I should have known you didn't send that letter."

She snorted. "All together? Yeah, well, I'm good at being

fake. What can I say?"

"You don't have to be fake with me, Donna."

She sniffled, and wiped her nose on the sleeve of her shirt. "You're always so nice, Laura. I'm so sorry about everything that's happened lately. How have you coped? You always seem so upbeat."

That was news to me. "I guess I just try to trust God that all things happen for a purpose. Sometimes it's hard to trust him, though. I don't always do a great job."

She locked gazes with me for a moment. "That's what's different about you. You're the real thing, aren't you?"

My heart lurched. "What do you mean?"

"You're really a Christian, not just someone who goes to church."

I swallowed, not sure if I lived up to her statement or not. "That's how I try to live. I'll be praying for you, Donna."

A faint smile touched her lips. "Thank you. You can pray for Tiara, too. She's been having a hard time lately. She feels guilty that she was so mean to Candace before she died."

I leaned closer. "Mean to her how?"

"Well, she was mad at Candace because Tiara knew about her threats to reveal my criminal past, so Tiara started this petition to have the Flynns kicked out of the neighborhood for not following the bylaws. But then Candace died."

"You guys used to all be friends, didn't you?"

"Yeah. It's funny how quickly relationships can go south."

Didn't I know it. If I wasn't careful, Kent and I would end up all the way at the bottom of that pit.

I stood. "You have a good lawyer, don't you?"

She nodded.

"I don't think they're going to be able to keep you here for this crime, Donna. That's a totally unprofessional opinion, of course, but I hope you get out soon."

"I didn't send you that banana bread. You know that, don't you?"

"I do." And right then, I did. Someone was trying to set Donna up.

"Maybe I should try a bit of that prayer sometime." She reached her hand out. "Thanks for coming by to visit. It means a lot. Not many people have been so brave."

※※※

I decided to walk to the pharmacy and see how things were going there. Kent was meeting with the insurance adjustor. After talking with Donna, I felt a renewed sense of purpose. When I found Kent, I was even smiling. Too bad he wasn't.

"This is just a mess. I don't understand why someone would do this." His head swung around as he surveyed the shattered glass, overturned shelves, and holes in the wall.

I put my arms around him. "I'm so sorry, honey. How can I help?"

"They said we could start cleaning up," Kent said. "I just don't even know where to start. I'm going to have to get this store looking halfway decent if I expect to sell it. I just can't leave it like this. Besides, people have prescriptions they need. All that information was in my computer. I'll have to get in touch with doctor's offices and other pharmacies. It's going to be a headache."

I kissed his cheek. "You do that and I'll start cleaning up what I can. How does that sound?"

"You're going to be working for weeks cleaning up this place."

I grabbed a broom from the rack where they used to be sold. "That's okay. I'll manage, one sweep at a time."

Kent climbed over things until he reached the pharmacy counter. He also had to count his medications to see what had been stolen. This would be a big task. For insurance purposes, I had to record all the damaged merchandise I found.

I was still working on the first shelf when I heard someone walk in through the front door. I turned around and saw Babe. I quickly stood and wiped the dirt from my jeans. "Babe, what are you doing here?"

"I'm sorry about everything that's happened, Laura. I just feel awful that someone did this to your store."

"Thanks. I appreciate you stopping by, especially considering our last conversation. I'm sorry I was so insensitive."

"You're forgiven."

I smiled as she stepped over an avalanche of canned beans and hugged me.

"Now, what can I do to help?"

My spirits suddenly lifted. "You want to help?"

"Of course. That's what friends are for."

Harry poked his head in a few minutes later and ended up scrubbing graffiti from the storefront. By six o'clock, it seemed like half of the town had stopped by to help out in some way.

Maybe Boring wasn't so bad after all.

When we were all done and everyone had left, Kent and I sat back and stared at the place. Aside from the boards over the windows, it didn't look half bad.

"Maybe this won't take as long as I expected."

"No, people were really great today, weren't they?"

"Yeah, I finally felt like I was a true Boring resident."

He echoed my thoughts exactly. Today, I'd been proud to live in Boring. I don't know what we would have done without everyone's help.

I rested my cheek against his arm. "I love you."

He kissed the top of my head. "I love you too." Suddenly, he stood. "You want a sandwich?"

"Are you going to make it?" I raised my eyebrows.

"I've made a few sandwiches in my day."

"Not since we've been married."

"I feigned ignorance."

I slapped my hand against my knee before pointing at my husband. "I knew it! What bachelor can't make grilled cheese sandwiches?"

He grinned like a school boy. "One grilled cheese coming up."

I watched as Kent rolled up his sleeves and began pulling

things from the refrigerator. He even pulled a white apron over his outfit and acted like he would flip the sandwiches with his spatula. He turned on a little radio and sang along to "Can't Buy Me Love." I don't remember the last time I laughed so hard.

Finally, he sat down at the bar beside me with a plateful of sandwiches.

"Can I get you a drink?"

"What do you have?"

"The finest selection of soda pop this side of the Mississippi." He bowed gracefully and displayed a soda as if it was an expensive bottle of wine. He said it all with a terrible French accent. "This one was made in 2012, and shipped here all the way from the ultra exotic land of Ohio."

I giggled. "I'll take that."

He popped the top and set it on the counter. "You know what?"

I turned to him and wiped a strand of cheese from my lip. "What?"

"Everything is so much more bearable with you by my side."

I wanted to melt. Those were just about the sweetest words he'd ever said to me. "Really?"

"Absolutely."

"Oh, Kent, that's just about the nicest thing you've told me since—since we moved here, I guess."

He brushed a hair behind my ear. "I know it's been hard on you. It will get better. I'll get better."

"Who said there was room for improvement?"

He nudged my chin. "You didn't need to. I can see it all over your face."

I touched my cheek. "Really? I thought I was a better faker than that."

"That's what's so charming about you—you think you're good at being fake, but you're not. It's so obvious."

"Really?"

He nodded with soft eyes. "Really. But that's what I love about you. Even when you try to put on a mask, you can't. You're too genuine."

Maybe this was when I should ask him about his Friday afternoon outings. "Kent, there's something I want to ask—"

A kiss cut me off.

Oh, no. I had to get this out. "Kent, really—"

We were kissing again. I shouldn't complain. I wasn't complaining. But still, there was that dirty little issue of his secret.

He suddenly stood and intertwined his fingers with mine. "Let's go home."

"But your sandwich?"

"I'm not hungry anymore."

The next day was Boring's annual Ginseng Festival. They closed down the entire downtown area so vendors could set up booths. In the high school parking lot, amusements had been pitched. Various local performers showed off their talents, including Emma Jean, who apparently could play a mean harmonica.

Kent and I decided to check out the festival, just for kicks. Maybe we'd even try a cup of that ginseng ice cream we'd heard so much about. We spent most of the morning looking at the work of various artists and chatting with townspeople about the pharmacy. We didn't mention to anyone that we'd be moving. I figured we'd wait until closer to the time. Babe joined us for awhile, though she looked distracted. Her eyes kept scanning the crowd.

"Is everything okay?"

She nodded. "Just seeing who's here. Making sure everyone is down with the Ginseng Festival."

"You really like this festival, don't you?"

"Look forward to it every year."

"Why?"

"Ginseng is a part of this town. It helps to put food in people's mouths. It brings people together."

Babe finally saw someone in the distance and hurried toward them. "I'll catch you later!"

I wondered who she'd been so anxious to find. Of course, all kinds of people who'd moved away from the town came back for this festival.

By the time we made it over to the rides, it was dark outside. Why they had this event in the winter was beyond me—but no one had asked my opinion. I couldn't really imagine riding The Terminator while the wind cut through my clothing and chilled me to the bone.

Kent and I took our places to watch the lawnmower races on the high school football field, which was lit bright enough to compete with the sun. Steele, Darius, and Mark had all signed up.

"Why didn't you sign up, honey?"

"Maybe next year." His words stayed in my mind. We wouldn't be here next year at this time, but maybe we could make it a tradition to come back for the festival.

"Let me go get us a box of popcorn."

"Sounds great."

I stood near the halfway point and watched as all the men and the tough-as-nails fitness instructor Karen Jones lined up to start. I hoped Kent didn't miss the beginning. The announcer counted down, and the lawnmowers were off.

I cheered as I saw Darius taking the lead.

This was one thing we didn't have in Chicago. Of course, we did turn an entire river green in honor of St. Patrick's Day.

Mark—Hillary's husband—raced in front. I watched to see if Darius would be able to gain his lead back. They rounded the corner, headed to my side of the track. The crowds around me cheered.

A hand pressed on my back. Kent must have returned.

Just as I turned to say hi, someone shoved me. Hard.

I tumbled onto the race track, my hands colliding with the grass. I looked up just in time to see the lawn mowers headed right at me.

# 25

Panic pulled back the corners of my mouth. If Darius didn't move, he was going to mow right over me. I tried to roll out of the way but couldn't. Fear froze me.

Instead, I screamed. People in the crowd screamed.

I prepared for death, if a person can possibly do that.

I closed my eyes and waited to feel my bones being crushed under the weight of the machines.

Instead, I heard metal crunching. Men yelling. Women screaming.

Finally, I opened my eyes. I saw three lawn mowers piled up mere inches from me. Darius, Steele and Mark lay on the ground, rubbing their heads and elbows. In avoiding me, they hadn't been able to avoid each other.

People surrounded us. I forced myself to sit up and scan the crowd. Was the person who pushed me still watching? I searched for any retreating figures but saw none.

"Laura! What happened?" Kent knelt beside me, a knot between his eyebrows as he grasped my arms.

"Someone pushed me." My eyes continued to scan the people around me. Leaning on Kent, I rose to my feet. "Did anyone see who did this?" I asked loudly.

"See who did what?" Emma Jean asked.

"Who pushed me in front of the lawn mowers?"

The crowd gasped in unison.

Kent continued to hold me up, his hands grasping my arms. "Are you sure someone pushed you?"

"You bet your poisoned pork rinds."

"It was so crowded," Emma Jean said. "Anyone could have done it."

I locked eyes with the woman. Emma Jean had been beside me. She might hate city slickers, but was she a killer?

I glanced at the men as they brushed themselves off. They all seemed uninjured, thank goodness. The outcome could have been much worse. I'm sure that's what the person who'd tried to kill me had wanted.

Whoever did this was getting more desperate. That must mean I was getting closer to the truth.

"Honey, we better get you home." Kent tried to lead me away.

Someone cleared his throat beside us. "Right after we question her. Again."

I would know that voice anywhere. Chief Romeo. He stood poised with his pen and paper in hand and a look of "haven't we been here before" all over his face.

My thoughts exactly.

※※※

Kent and I decided to spend the rest of the evening at home, relaxing. Since it was the week before the Super Bowl, there were no football games on TV. That meant Kent had to watch reruns of Law & Order with me.

As we were resting on the couch, the phone rang. It was my mother. She only called a few times a year to check on me, and lately I'd been hoping she wouldn't.

My parents had high hopes for me—success to them was defined in material possessions, climbing the corporate ladder, and staying fit. For my entire life, I'd pushed myself to make them proud.

They still didn't know the real reason I'd left my job in Chicago. They thought I quit to move to Boring. I knew that one day the truth would come out. I hoped today was not that day.

"How's the pharmacy?" my mother asked. I pondered what to say.

"It's, uh, it's okay." Ransacked, vandalized and about to be sold, but okay.

"Have you found a new job yet?"

"Haven't really looked."

"It's 'I haven't really looked.' You're beginning to speak as if I raised you to be uncivilized and uncultured."

"Sorry." I bit my lip. "I mean, I'm sorry."

"I can't believe your old firm wouldn't let you work from home. That's the new thing, you know. Telecommuting. You should talk to them about that. I bet they would work something out with you. In the long run, it would save them money on office space."

"It's something to think about."

"Or maybe your husband will realize the futility of working in a small town and come to his senses."

"Living in a small town doesn't make you less of a person, Mom."

"It makes you closed minded. There's so much more out there."

"But the more that's out there isn't necessarily better." Why was I defending small town life? It was so unlike me.

The conversation continued for ten more minutes until I finally told my mother I had a headache and needed to go to bed. It was the truth. Talking to my mother always gave me a headache.

She thought that marrying Kent made me weak. She never said it, but I got the message loud and clear. She was an agnostic, and Kent was the one who'd introduced me to Christ. At first, I'd gone to church with him simply because we were dating and I wanted to make a good impression. But slowly the beliefs I'd learned there had begun to make sense. I'd become a Christian. I don't think my mother had ever forgiven me for it.

"You okay?" Kent asked.

"I'm exhausted."

"It's been a long day." He put his hand on my knee. "I don't like everything's that's been going on lately. I feel like you were safer in Chicago than you are here in Boring."

I forced a smile. "Strange, isn't it?"

He frowned. "I had higher expectations for small town life. Maybe I just had to get this dream out of my system so I could move on. I'm just sorry you had to get hurt in the process."

"Life's a learning experience."

"I'll call a realtor tomorrow about putting the house on the market. How's that sound?"

I smiled. "Sounds great."

※※※

I couldn't stop looking at the "For Sale" sign in my front yard. Just the sight of it made me feel giddy, even in the grey of dusk.

I was finally going to get out of Dodge.

I was standing in the front yard looking at it when I felt someone behind me.

"You're really moving, chickaroonie? You're leaving Boring? You're selling your crib?"

I looked behind me at Babe. "Kent and I both think it's time, especially in light of everything that's happened lately."

"The pharmacy can be fixed, you know."

"It can, but is it worth it? You know, Kent and I gave it a shot here, but maybe Emma Jean is right. We're both city slickers at heart."

"You're letting them win."

I stopped looking at the sign for a minute. "I'm letting who win?"

"Whoever is trying to drive you out of town."

"The decision is inevitable. It would have happened eventually, with or without everything that's happened lately. Kent and I just aren't cut out for small town life. And that's okay."

"I think you are cut out for life here. You just never gave it a chance."

"Babe, you're one of the only reasons I'm going to miss about being here."

"I'm surprised you're leaving things unfinished like this."

"What's unfinished?"

"Candace's murder."

"Like I'm going to figure out who did that."

"You're obviously getting close. Someone wants you to stop snooping."

I sighed. "I've thought of that. But I'm out of ideas. It's time for me to let go of this amateur detective thing."

"I never took you as a quitter."

I scowled. "There's a difference between quitting and moving on. You have to have wisdom to discern between those two things. I'm moving on."

Babe pointed in the distance. "Isn't that Harry McCoy's truck over at the Brunos'?"

I glanced over. "He's been over there a lot lately."

"I wonder why. What could he have in common with that family?"

"Good question."

We both stared at the house for a moment.

I remembered seeing Harry that first night Babe and I had patrol duty alone. He'd had dirt all over his clothes and said he was looking for his keys, yet his front door was wide open.

I remembered him whispering with Steele Bruno.

I remembered his vendetta against Jerry.

And when all the other men in town had been racing lawn mowers, Harry was watching from the crowds. He could have pushed me. I don't care how convincing he'd been when I talked to him at the pharmacy. The fact still remained that he could be guilty. He worked for the cable company. Maybe he'd been in the Flynns' house before to do some work and had snagged a copy of their house key. He'd even been in our house to hook up our wireless Internet. Maybe that's how he'd left the banana bread or listening device. In fact, Harry could pretty much have access to any house he wanted in the neighborhood.

"What are they doing in their back yard? I keep seeing dirt fly in the air." I squinted and leaned closer.

"Maybe they're burying something." Babe paused. "Like another dead body."

My eyes widened. "Babe!"

"Well, they have been acting suspicious."

I continued to watch the dirt fly. "Maybe we should check it out."

Babe and I crept toward the Bruno house. Maybe I would finish solving this mystery before I left, after all.

We tiptoed to the fence. I peeked between the cracks in the pickets. I could clearly see Harry and Darius digging a narrow trench in the ground. The unearthed dirt was too small for a body. What could they be burying? Evidence? Babe and I looked at each other.

"You sure we're not going to get caught?" Steele asked, wiping the sweat from his brow.

"People do this all the time. It's no big deal. No one will ever know."

"Yeah, last time you said that the power in the entire neighborhood went out."

So, Harry had caused that power outage? What exactly were they doing?

One thing I did know was that Harry and Steele both were large men who could easily take down Babe and me. Maybe we should get out of here and call the police. I'm sure Chief Romeo would be more than happy to hear another one of my theories.

"We should go," I whispered to Babe.

We turned around just in time to see Gia standing behind us, a knife in hand.

"I wish you hadn't seen that," Gia said, shaking her head.

# 26

"We didn't see anything," Babe insisted.

I shook my head and backed against the fence. The fence. Could I the scale the privacy in order to save my life? Could Babe? "Not a thing."

Gia stepped closer, the knife glistening under the illumination of a nearby streetlight that just flickered on. "We're not doing anything wrong."

My throat felt as dry as the wooden fence at my fingertips. "We never said you were."

Gia shook her head, flailing the knife in front of her as she spoke. "It's just that this Homeowners' Association has all of these crazy rules. They're driving me mad!"

What did the Homeowners' Association have to do with killing us? Now wasn't the time to ask. Instead, I wanted to be on her side, to let Gia know I wasn't a threat. "They can be maddening."

She sighed and flung her hand in the air, the knife with it. "We knew Hillary would never approve."

I continued to stare at the weapon in her hands. I willed myself to keep my voice steady. "Of murder? Who does approve of that?"

Gia put her hands on her hips, pointing the knife away from us for once. Her eyes widened. Her lips parted. "Murder? What are you talking about? Are you crazy?"

"You're the one with the knife." I nodded toward the weapon.

Gia held it up and laughed. "I was just chopping up veggies to snack on when I saw you out the kitchen window."

I let out a weak laugh, still not a hundred-percent relaxed. "So—that's not a weapon?"

She snorted. "A weapon? Get real. Who do you think I am? A killer?" She laughed, a little too loudly.

"There was a murder in the neighborhood," Babe pointed out.

I nodded. "And your husband is burying something in the backyard."

"Cable! He's burying a cable line in the back yard."

Babe and I looked at each other in horror.

"You mean, they're stealing cable? That's what all of this is about?" I had to laugh.

"We're not stealing it. We're setting up a screen in our backyard so we can watch movies out there in the summer with our pals from the city. I knew Hillary would never approve, so we went behind her back. Harry is helping us to set things up."

"What about the power outage?"

She snorted again. "The first time the two brainiacs tried to do it, they dug too deep and cut a line. That's what they get for trying to do it at night."

"Who are you talking to, honey?" Steele opened the gate and stopped cold. "This isn't what it looks like." He dropped his shovel.

Harry appeared behind him. "Don't tell Hillary. Please. I don't want her to slap me with a fine for breaking the association's rules."

"We won't tell Hillary," Babe said. "As long as you invite us over for a movie when it gets warmer."

Gia and Steele grinned. "It's a deal."

I watched Steele and Harry interact. "I'm curious—how do you two know each other?"

"We met in college. Harry's been trying to talk us into moving here for a long time. Said it was a great place to raise a family."

"I wanted somewhere else to buy a couch. That one Jerry sold me was horrible and then he wouldn't let me return it."

"Did that make you mad?"

"Of course it did."

"Mad enough to kill him?" Yeah, we'd had this conversation before. Maybe it was time to revisit it, though.

"Of course it didn't! I don't get mad. I get even. That's why I'm helping Steele open up a Futon World store here in Boring."

Gia leaned closer. "Now that you're in on our little secret, how about you come over tonight to test out the screen?"

"Isn't it a little cold outside to be watching movies?"

"We hooked up surround sound into our sun room. We can sit in there and watch whatever we want, just like on the big screen." She held up her knife. "We're having veggies and wings."

We all laughed.

"We'll be there," Babe and I said in unison.

***

I read the text across the massive screen attached to the Brunos' fence. "What show is this clip from?"

Part of a TV program flashed across the white.

Kent hit the buzzer. "*Battlestar Galactica!*"

His answer was right, as it had been the last six times. Everyone on our team cheered and stood up to give Kent a high five.

Babe, Tiara, and Darius were all on our team.

We faced off against the Brunos, Harry and the Jones family from two streets over. So far, we were winning.

I had to admit, playing the pop culture trivia game on the big screen was a lot of fun. There was also a surge of excitement in knowing we were breaking the association rules.

But the one thing I'd learned during the course of the evening was that Kent was even more of a couch potato than I'd realized. Only someone who watched a lot of TV could know the things he did.

Growing up, my parents had emphasized what a waste of time TV was. There were more important things one could be doing, things like studying, putting in community service hours—which looked great on your resume and college applications—and job shadowing people in order to gain more experience for the future.

My parents were very goal oriented.

Maybe that thinking had been ingrained in me; knowing that Kent liked to mindlessly watch TV so much made me feel uneasy.

We took a break from the game to grab more snacks.

"So, you guys are really moving," Tiara said, while grabbing a stick of celery. "What about the pharmacy?"

"We'll put it up for sale after it's cleaned up." I crunched on a carrot. "It's a shame someone had to mess up the place."

"It's a shame you're selling it. We're going to miss you here."

My face flushed. "You are?"

Gia stepped up from behind. "We are going to miss you. We hardly had a chance to get to know you. Plus, I was hoping to get some advice on how to adjust to small town life after coming from the city."

I half-shrugged. "I can't say I ever adjusted."

"I can't say that Boring is my ideal for a place to live, but I can say that I don't miss the city at all."

I took another carrot stick. "Not at all?"

"I like the slower pace. Gives you more time to think, more time to discover who you are. I would have never thought I liked small town fairs, but I had so much fun yesterday."

Steele stepped forward. "I have to say that I'm impressed by all the people who already know my name."

I remembered the hustle and bustle of the city. How my days were filled with activities—mostly work. When I wasn't working, I was busy doing other things, like going to nice dinners or shows. I guess it was easy to forget who you were when you never had time to examine your life.

Here in Boring, I was no longer a public relations executive. I was just Laura Berry. Who was Laura Berry, though? Did I really know?

"Let's go start round two, everyone!" Gia called us all back into the sunroom.

No sooner had we sat down to start playing did the doorbell ring.

Steele and Gia looked at each other. "Did you invite anyone else?" Gia asked.

Steele shook his head. "You?"

"No, I sure didn't."

The doorbell rang again. Everyone quieted as the Brunos hurried to the door.

I heard Hillary's voice all the way into the sunroom.

"What is that thing in the backyard? Don't you know you have to have approval to put something like that in your backyard? Anything that your neighbors can see needs to be approved. Did you not read that in the association rules?"

"We must have skipped that section," I heard Steele say.

"What am I going to tell your neighbors when they ask me about this? I'm responsible for this neighborhood. We have rules for a reason."

"Well, why don't you ask them now?" Steele said.

The three of them rounded the corner. Hillary stopped in her tracks when she saw all of us sitting in the sunroom. "You all knew about this? I thought you were responsible citizens. I thought you cared about this neighborhood. I thought you respected the rules!"

I felt about the size of an ant. She seemed to zero her gaze in on me as she spoke. I was the temporary treasurer of the association. Perhaps I should have acted more responsibly. I shifted in my chair and looked away.

"You're being ridiculous, Hillary," Babe said. "No one on the cul-de-sac cares."

"Oh, no one, you say? We'll see about that! If I find one objection, you're going to have to take it down."

"Or else what?" Steele asked.

Hillary's eyes fired up even more. "Or else we'll begin litigation, and I'll make sure you're kicked out of this neighborhood. I was very clear when I wrote the bylaws, just in case an incident like this happened. Rules are made for a reason."

She looked at me one more time before storming out of the house. As soon as she left, everyone looked at each other in silence.

"Is she for real?" Gia asked.

Harry grimaced. "Unfortunately."

"This is why Donna should be president," Tiara said.

"Donna? Isn't she the one who's locked up for killing that lady?" Gia said.

Tiara shook her head so hard that her dangling earrings slapped her cheeks. "She didn't do it. She's being framed."

"Laura, aren't you friends with Hillary?" Gia asked. "Will you see if you can talk some sense into her? The last thing we need right now is a lawsuit. And can she really kick us out of the neighborhood?"

"I doubt it." I shrugged, suddenly even more uncomfortable. "As far as talking to her, I don't know if I'd say we were friends—"

"You're more her friend than anyone else in this room," Babe pointed out. I saw a sparkle in her eyes. "Besides, what do you have to lose? You're moving anyway."

"If I have the chance, I'll say something to her tomorrow." I looked at Gia. "She's not really as bad as you think. She just likes things to be orderly."

"Maybe she killed Candace. Did you ever think of that?" Tiara asked.

I shrugged. "She has an alibi. She was at a banquet up in Indy with her husband. Besides, just because she's militant doesn't mean she's capable of killing."

"Now that that's covered, how about we move on to round two?" Kent asked.

Yes, why don't we move on to show everyone what a big TV nerd you are.

Tomorrow was our anniversary. I wondered what Kent had planned. He hadn't mentioned anything, but I figured if we did anything it would be in the afternoon. After all, the Super Bowl was tomorrow. I might expect him to be a good husband but not a saint. I hadn't made as much progress as I'd hoped on his man cave. With us moving, I figured I shouldn't pursue those plans any more. Maybe we could get an extra bedroom in our new Chicago apartment, and he could use that for his own place. I had the couch I'd purchased waiting for pick up at the store.

Kent buzzed in again and stood up, as if unable to contain his excitement.

"*King of Queens*! The *King of Queens* features a main character who likes to watch TV!"

Everyone on our team cheered.

How appropriate. Why did I feel like my life was that sitcom right now?

⁂

"Tonight is the big game. Best day of the year." Kent had the nerve to wear his team's colors to church. As he rambled on and on about the game, I thought over and over about how he hadn't mentioned our anniversary yet.

He couldn't have forgotten, right? I mean, things had gotten better between us lately. I hated to think it, but ever since the pharmacy had been vandalized, Kent and I had been closer. Probably because we had more time to spend together.

But here it was our seven-year anniversary, and he hadn't

even mentioned it yet.

Of course, neither had I, but that was only because I was waiting for him to mention it first. I already had my card bought, a nice note written inside and signed with love. I'd wait until he presented me with his card before I gave him mine.

Kent never forgot anything, especially not anything important. So I knew he didn't forget our seven years together.

All through church, he didn't mention it.

All during lunch, he didn't bring it up.

He did, however, bring up the Super Bowl. Over and over.

Then I kept thinking about the proof I'd received last night that he was truly a couch potato. Yes, we definitely needed to move back to Chicago. Better yet, maybe we should move to a remote village where TVs didn't exist. Would that solve our problems?

Or was the TV really the source of our problems at all?

Megan called me after lunch.

"Congrats on seven years together. What are you and Kent doing to celebrate?"

I scowled, though she couldn't see me. "We're watching the Super Bowl. Or, as I like to say, we're celebrating the end of football season for another year."

"How romantic."

I scowled again. "Tell me about it."

"Have you thought any more about my offer?"

I pounded up the stairs, a moment of adrenaline surging through me. "I have. And I'd love to go in with you to start our own PR firm. We've already put our house on the market."

Of course, the more time I worked at my own company, the less time Kent and I would have together. I shoved that thought to the back of my mind. He'd be busy working at the pharmacy anyway. And he always had the TV to keep him company. My heart panged at the thought, though.

We talked about our plans together. I'd go up at the end of next week to meet with her and sign the paperwork.

When we hung up, Babe called.

"Are you going to the party at Hillary's?" I asked. Of course, I wasn't sure I was really invited anymore, not after last night. But since I hadn't been officially uninvited, I figured I'd go. It beat staying home alone on a day I should be celebrating my marriage. Kent would be at Darius's house with a group of men from the neighborhood.

"No, I need to meet with Paul to discuss the financial security of my future."

"Babe, is everything okay? Are you having money problems?"

"No, no. It's nothing like that. It's just that I've been needing to meet with him but putting it off. It turns out neither of us have any interest in watching the Super Bowl, so we decided to meet tonight."

"Why not during business hours?" It all seemed a little strange to me.

"He'll be out of town this week. Besides, he's not acting as the president of the bank. He's just doing this for me to be nice."

"But I thought you hated him."

"Hated is a strong word. He is the only banker in town, Laura."

Maybe I would never figure Babe out.

We got off the phone, and I went over to my desk to find the card I'd purchased for Kent. I saw a paper sticking out from a stack and pulled it out. My scribbles about suspects and clues.

Who was I to think I could solve Candace's murder? Every guess I'd had was wrong. But I did know that Donna wasn't guilty—she was locked up when someone pushed me in front of that lawn mower. The killer was still out there.

Maybe moving away from Boring was the only way to preserve my life.

I crumpled the paper and threw it in the trash. It was time for me to move on.

# 27

Kent slipped into his Chicago Bears' jacket and kissed my forehead. "Thanks for letting me go to the Super Bowl party, honey. This is going to be the game of the year."

I nodded, my throat tightening. I still couldn't believe Kent had forgotten our anniversary. Even if everything else in life was going wrong, if my marriage still gave me hope, then I knew I'd be okay. But for Kent to forget our anniversary—what did this say about our marriage?

I nodded as he took off for Darius's place. Then I donned my own jacket so I could drive to Hillary's. I wasn't looking forward to her annual "Souper Bowl Spa Party." Not only did I not want to see Hillary again, I also didn't want to ask her about the screen as I'd promised Steele I would do. Mostly, I just wanted to stay home and feel sorry for myself.

I plastered on a smile when I walked into the party. A lot of the women from the neighborhood were already here. I doubted most of them wanted to be here—Hillary really didn't have any friends. They were probably here hoping to get on her good side so she'd be a little more lenient with them should they break the association rules. My mom had always told me I should be in good graces with the people who held the power.

Hillary had little centers set up all over her house. In the dining room, people were doing their nails. In the living room, a professional masseuse gave back rubs. In the TV room, a romantic comedy played. And, of course, in the kitchen, there were a variety of soups—everything from broccoli and cheese to gazpacho.

I chatted with Tiara and Karen Jones, and even briefly with Emma Jean.

I really wished Babe were here. I wanted to pour my heart out to someone about how Kent had forgotten our anniversary. I didn't realize how much I'd come to depend on Babe as a confidante.

Tears rushed to my eyes at the thought of leaving her behind. Even though I complained about our adventures, Babe had added a lot of fun to my time here in Boring. I'd miss her terribly when I moved. I hadn't had any good friends in Chicago, friends I trusted enough to share the really important stuff with.

I needed to get to a bathroom to compose myself, I realized, as tears threatened to escape. I tried the one downstairs but someone was using it. I didn't think Hillary would mind if I used the upstairs one. I padded up the steps and away from the noise of the party. After clearing the landing, I passed two doors before seeing the bathroom in the distance. Voices behind one of the doors caused me to stop.

"I'm tired of pretending, Hillary. We can't keep this up much longer."

"You will keep pretending! Our money troubles are no one's business. As far as they know, we've got everything together."

I stepped into the bathroom, knowing I shouldn't listen to Hillary and her husband argue. Yet, I couldn't help it. Their hushed whispers weren't soft enough.

"We can't continue living at our current level. We're just setting ourselves up for an even bigger and more public failure if we do." Hillary's husband sounded weary.

It was good, in one way, to know that other couples had their problems too. Yet, I hated it sometimes when I realized that life was never as easy as I'd like.

Their secret would be safe with me. I sure wouldn't want Kent's and my dirty laundry to be aired for the whole neighborhood.

When I returned downstairs, I tried to pay attention to the girl talk around me as we painted our fingernails and scrubbed the dead skin cells from our feet. After hearing Hillary and Mark talk about their financial problems, my mind continually wandered back to the association's books. Why did I have the feeling the answers waited for me there? Answers that would get Donna out of jail and put the right man or woman where they belonged?

I just needed to look at the ledger one more time. Surely I

could figure out what was nagging at the back of my mind.

I stood, causing the cucumber slices to fall from my eyes. Thankfully, the other women couldn't see me because of their own vegetable-covered lids.

"Ladies, I just remembered that I need to run home and check on something. I'll be right back."

"Can't it wait?" Gia asked.

I wanted to lie and say something about a candle that I'd left burning or something. But I couldn't do that. I wouldn't add lying to my list of things of which to be ashamed. "No, actually, it can't. I really must run right now. I should only be gone a moment, though."

It wasn't until I was outside that I realized I still had the avocado mask slathered on my face. If I talked too much, it would crack. Hopefully, I wouldn't see too many people while I was out since everyone was either watching the Super Bowl or avoiding it. I'd wait to wash it off. After all, I was going back to the party. Why ruin a perfectly good moisturizing treatment?

The cold air outside caused my mask to instantly tighten and feel even more tingly than before. I fished my keys from my pocket and rushed to my car. The drive home only took a few minutes. I glanced across the street at Tiara's house and saw all the lights on. I imagined the men inside eating nachos and popcorn and rooting for their favorite teams.

I glanced at our own garage, where I'd planned to surprise Kent with his man cave. Now I might just cancel my order for that stupid couch, even if I lost money in the process. I don't know why I ever thought the man cave was a good idea. I should simply resign myself to a loveless marriage for the rest of my days. Since I didn't believe in divorce, that seemed the only alternative.

I hurried inside the house, catching a sniff of the apple-scented air fragrance I'd plugged in earlier. Well, at least I did that right. I may not be a housekeeper, but I knew how to make things smell good.

Seemed an appropriate job description for someone who used to work in public relations.

I ran upstairs to my bedroom, where I'd left the file on the homeowners' association's treasury. I crunched the numbers again. Math may not have been my strongest subject in school, but I did have an eye for detail. Something wasn't adding up.

Sure, the association had paid its regular bills for the maintenance of the pond and lawn care. But the statement I'd picked up from the bank clearly reflected a lower account balance than our records showed.

Candace had been the only one with authority to write checks. Had she been stealing money? Who else could be taking it?

One face stood out in my mind.

# 28

I jumped into my SUV and took off toward the bank. I hastily threw my vehicle into park on the street and rushed to the door. Relief filled me when the door easily opened. Mr. Willis really needed to make sure his doors were locked, but right now that worked in my favor. Inside, the lights glared and soft music played overhead. I saw no one.

The office! They had to be in the office. I hurried across the tile floor, my heart racing erratically. I flew down the hallway, caught the door facing, and swung myself into the room in a way that would make any detective proud.

Two heads bobbed on the couch. One wearing a fedora, and the other stylishly white.

I open my mouth to speak when I realized what I'd walked in on. Babe and Paul—kissing?

Oh, my eyes.

Perhaps it was my sharp intake of breath that gave me away. Babe stood and squinted at me.

"Laura? What is wrong with you? What's on your face?"

"My face?" I touched my cheek and felt the avocado mask. "Oh, that. It's nothing.

"You look like you've been through a tornado."

I caught my breath and shook my head. "Wait. You two. Together?"

Babe blushed, and looked with glowing eyes at Paul. "We can't deny our feelings anymore."

Great, my best friend had found love again—with a killer. I extended a cautious hand, determined to make Babe understand the seriousness of the situation. With a steady voice, I said, "Babe, I think you should step away from Paul."

"Why would I do that, Laura?" Babe blinked her eyes at me innocently.

Paul's brows furrowed together, and he tipped his hat back so I could better see his eyes. "Yes, why would she do that?"

I reached my hand out toward her, as if I were in a lifeboat and she were drowning. "Babe, just listen to me. Come over here with me. And whatever you do, don't eat that cake."

Babe's eyebrows shot up. "I didn't think you drank alcohol."

I paused. "What? I don't."

"You're acting like you're three sheets to the wind."

Irritation threatened to boil over, but I managed to keep my tone even. "Babe, Paul killed Candace."

At that, Paul released Babe—or maybe she released him, not

sure—and they stepped apart, looking suspiciously at each other.

"What are you talking about, girl? I didn't kill anyone!" His hands went to his hips.

"You're the only one besides Candace who had access to the association's treasury. You've been stealing funds, and Candace found out. You had to keep her quiet."

"Why in the world would I steal from that measly little treasury, little girl? I have enough money that I don't have to work—I do it because I like to."

Good point. I couldn't let that logic deter me, though. He was the only one with access. Paul had to be the killer.

I pointed at him and took a step back, just in case he had any tricks up his sleeve. "Maybe it's just for the thrill of seeing what you can get away with."

"He didn't do it, Laura." Babe stepped into the crook of his arm.

I shook my head, trying to warn her to stay back. She didn't listen. How could Babe not trust me, after everything we'd been through together? Besides, I thought she despised Paul. I guessed that sometimes love and hate could look an awful lot alike.

Babe, this theory is the only thing that makes sense. He did it!" I tried to beckon her with my eyes. "Please believe me."

Paul threw his free hand in the air. I could see he was frustrated. "We were discussing bankruptcy, you foolish girl! The store isn't doing well, in case you haven't heard. I was giving her some options."

I shrugged. "A likely story."

"Besides," Babe looked at the floor. When she glanced back up, I think I saw her blush. "He has an alibi."

"Who?"

"Me. Paul and I were together on the night Candace died, having dinner."

My mouth gapped open. "You two have been seeing each other that long? I thought you hated each other."

Babe tilted her head to the side and said matter-of-factly, "Certain things are best left private, Laura. I didn't want everyone in this town knowing my business. Besides, I had to play hard to get. No man wants a woman who chases him."

I couldn't believe my ears. How had I missed this? Some detective I'd turned out to be. I'd think about this romance later. Now, I had to figure out who killed Candace. The answer was at my fingertips. I could feel it.

I leaned against the doorframe, suddenly exhausted. "Well, who else could have stolen the money? The figures definitely don't add up—you don't have to be a math expert to figure that out."

"There's only one other person authorized to access the account." Paul locked his gaze with mine.

My ears perked, as my hope surged. "And who's that?"

Paul looked at me like I should know the answer.

And right then, I did. I threw my head back and groaned. "How could I have missed that person?" The answer had been right in front of my eyes the whole time.

# 29

I passed Hillary's house on the way home and saw that the party was still in full swing. Silhouettes congregated behind the window shades, cars lined the street, and nearly every window was lit.

I had to get those record books before I went to the police station with my claims. Paul and Babe were already on their way there to back up my story.

I threw my car into park in my driveway and ran into my house. I didn't bother to turn the lights on. I had one goal: get the ledgers and leave. I had no time to waste.

My fingers ran over the table by my entryway, the place where I'd deposited those records. I felt the rough edges of a terracotta pot and the feathery wisps of the fern spilling over its sides. I felt the smooth line of the candy dish, filled with chocolate. But no books.

"Are you looking for these?"

I gasped at the strange voice in my house. Hillary.

I looked up and saw her form in the distance, waving the books in one hand and firmly grasping a gun in the other.

My throat went dry. I had to play it cool. "Hillary, what are you doing here? I thought you were at the spa party."

She stepped closer and narrowed her eyes. "I saw you leave and followed you. That's when I overheard your conversation with Babe. Figuring out who killed Candace took you longer than I anticipated. You're persistent, I'll give you that."

I held my hands in the air, feigning ignorance. "I don't know what you're talking about. I don't know anything. I was just about to go back to the party."

Hillary scowled. "You're an awful liar. You were going to the police. I can't let things end like this. I've worked too hard to get where I am."

I'd try the give-it-to-her-straight method now. "You did work hard to get to where you are. Why blow it by stealing from the treasury?"

"I have a certain standard of living, you know. How were we to know the housing market would dry up? Lenders—like Paul Willis—won't give us the money to develop new neighborhoods. Everyone thinks I've got it together. I couldn't let them know that we don't have the money to even pay our bills."

"But you're all about following rules. It's no wonder I didn't guess you killed Candace. How could you? Murder, Hillary?"

"She found out I'd been doctoring the books and began blackmailing me."

Blackmail? I didn't expect that.

"I couldn't let her go to the cops, but I couldn't afford to pay her anymore, either. Killing her was my only choice. I tried to make it as painless as possible. The little witch didn't even deserve that. She made my life miserable."

"There's no way you can cover up killing me, too, Hillary. Babe and Paul know you did it. They're probably telling the police now." Please, God, let them be telling the police now. I needed to buy more time. "I thought you were up in Indy on the day Candace died. The police said you had an alibi. People at the banquet saw you there."

"You certainly do your homework, now, don't you? I just made an appearance at that banquet. Then I slipped out, stopped by Candace's house to discuss a few things. I made sure she munched on those pork rinds while we spoke. Very few people knew she loved the things as much as she did—she'd just started a low-carb diet, and they were one of the few snacks she could eat. As soon as she slipped into sleep, I made sure she never ran her big mouth again."

"That's terrible."

"I made sure it looked like Donna did it. That was the easy part, as much as she always talked about those stupid cleaning cloths. She even gave me a sample, hoping I'd like them as much as she did. Little did she know I would really like them—as the murder weapon."

"How'd you know she used sleeping pills?"

Hillary shrugged. "I didn't. That just so happened to work out in my favor. About half of the population in the U.S. uses them at some point, so those statistics really worked in my favor."

"How'd you poison the pork rinds?"

"Easy. My husband had a master key made to all of your homes when he built this neighborhood. I could get into anyone's house whenever I wanted. Convenient, isn't it?" She sneered. "Any more questions, Mrs. I-can't-mind-my-own-business?"

"Why'd you stick the letter in Donna's mailbox instead of mine? I know you knew the difference."

She smiled as if I'd complimented her. "Easy. I wanted Donna's fingerprints to be found on the letter in case you turned it into the police."

"And the videotape? The bugging? They just don't make sense, Hillary."

Her smile slipped. "I wanted to make you paranoid. I wanted to make as many people as possible look guilty so I would look innocent. I studied to be a private detective several years ago. They taught me all about how to spy on someone."

"You were a private detective?"

"No, but I figured the information would come in handy one day. And it did. After I videoed you and set up that bug I just sat back to enjoy the show. The way you went all over town, searching for evidence, jumping at every little sound. People were beginning to think you'd lost it, Laura. That was all a part of my plan."

"And you wanted to make Donna look guilty? After the police had arrested her, you ransacked the pharmacy. Why would you do that?"

She shrugged, her eyes absent of emotion. "That's was just my way of trying to get you and your husband to leave town. I didn't realize how much fun I would end up having as I tried to ruin people's lives. I'm pretty good at it, it turns out."

"Killing me won't make anything easier for you, you know."

She nudged her gun in the air. "Everyone can see you're unhappy living in a small town, Laura. You tried to support your husband's dreams, but just couldn't take it anymore. You couldn't wait for your house to sell to get out of town. You had to leave now. That's what the note will say."

"What note?"

"The note you're going to write before I kill you and make you disappear."

I swallowed. The action hurt. "Even if you cover up my murder, you're still going to be charged with Candace's death."

"They can't prove it. Besides, a sudden job opportunity will mean that Mark and I have to move. I'll be long gone before this police department pieces together everything. When they look at the books, they'll see that you started doing them a few months ago—you should have read that paper I had you sign more carefully. All the evidence will point to you as the person responsible for her death. You were coming unhinged, dear. Everyone can see that."

I was coming unhinged? Everyone in the neighborhood knew that I'd just started as treasurer. I didn't bring that up, though. Instead, I stared at that gun. "You're making a mistake. No one's going to believe that."

"I guess I am. You said you were bad with numbers. That was the only reason I asked you to be treasurer. And the only reason I became your friend was to throw suspicion on other people. I underestimated you."

"I was voted most likely to succeed in high school."

She sneered. "That's not going to take you very far now, is it?"

"We can figure something out, Hillary. It doesn't have to end this way."

She walked past me, grabbing my arm as she did. "Come on. Let's go. To your car."

I couldn't get in the car with her. I'd learned enough through watching TV to know that I should never get in a car with someone with a gun. I'd likely die.

My only choice was to keep stalling.

"What about the note?"

She stopped, and her eyes narrowed. "You're going to email it." Her fingers clinched tighter into my arm. "Now come on, let's move. We don't have that much more time until the game is over."

Again, I'd be done in by football.

I tried to think of more reasons to stall, but my mind blanked. She jerked me toward the front door. "Say goodbye to this boring life you hated so much."

Suddenly, life in Boring seemed better than ever.

"Wait!"

Hillary's fiery gaze locked with mine. "What?"

Just then, the front door flew open, hitting Hillary in the head and pushing her toward me. I seized the moment and tried to grab her gun. Her grip was tight.

"Hello? Laura?"

Kent? What was he doing home? The game had to be in the last inning, or quarter, or whatever they called it.

Hillary regained her posture.

"Help!" I called.

"Hillary?" Confusion tinged Kent's voice.

Hillary almost had her gun back. Her finger played dangerously close to the trigger.

"Help, Kent!" I yelled again.

He grabbed Hillary. I twisted her arm until the gun began to slip from her grasp.

But not before a loud bang echoed in the foyer.

# 30

"Kent?" My voice sounded as tiny as a mouse.

"Laura?"

He didn't sound too far away. And he sounded alive, which was even better. Thank you, Lord. I reached forward until I felt his shirt and then pulled him closer, close enough that I could see his face in the inky darkness.

"Are you okay, Laura?"

My head throbbed, but other than that I appeared to be in one piece. I praised God again as I nodded. All that happened flashed back into my memory. The gun. Where was the gun? Where had the bullet ended up? "Where's the gun, Kent?"

Hillary groaned below us. Kent bolted toward the front door and flipped on the lights. As soon as he did, I spotted the pool of blood on the floor beneath Hillary's hand. I kicked the gun out of her reach, although I suspected she was in too much pain to grab it. Better safe than sorry, as the expression went.

A police siren sounded in the distance. Good. Help was coming. Babe and Paul had called the chief in time.

Kent's glance lingered on me. "What's on your face?"

I shrugged. "Just a beauty mask. I want to look pretty for you."

"You always look pretty to me."

I beamed, though he couldn't see it through the green on my skin. "That's so sweet."

"You stupid, stupid people," Hillary mumbled.

"I don't really need to explain who the stupid one here is, do I, Hillary?" I actually felt sorry for her. She'd been desperate, and desperate people did stupid things. Now she'd be paying for her decisions for a long time.

Hillary sneered at Kent, all the while grasping her injured hand. "You knew the whole time, didn't you? You were just playing games with me."

"Why would I know that you killed Candace? I don't ever talk to you." Kent's arm went around my waist, and he pulled me close.

"All those niceties that you kept saying to my husband and me whenever we went into your pharmacy, about how everything would be okay. God will get us through the tough times. Sharing your feelings can be freeing."

"I knew your husband was having troubles with his work. I wanted to encourage you both that things would work out eventually."

Her eyes squeezed shut in pain but, when she opened them

a moment later, bitterness had saturated her gaze. "How'd you know we were having financial problems?"

"He shared it with me one Friday after Fantasy Football. Apparently, he's been having a hard time. Your complaints have done nothing more than emasculate him."

She gasped. "He did? He shared that information? We both agreed to keep it quiet."

"He said he had to tell someone. Even men have to share their feelings sometime."

My mouth dropped open. "Fantasy Football? That's where you've been sneaking off to every Friday?" I couldn't help it—I laughed.

At least Kent had the decency to look embarrassed—and slightly confused. "It was actually a Fantasy Football group we formed. When we were doing our picks at the beginning of the season, we all had a great time together. We decided to meet every week for lunch at Harry's house. If your team lost, you had to bring the food. You knew about it?"

"Jasmine said you went somewhere every week." I shook my head. "The scenarios that went through my mind—"

"I'm sorry, honey. I should have told you. I just didn't think you'd approve."

Chief Romeo burst through the front door, gun drawn and sweat dripping from his face. Yeah, this was danger. Real danger. Not the video game sort. I wondered if Romeo had ever experienced that kind of fear in the line of duty while working here in Boring.

"I thought a key was appropriate. You hold the key to a lot of things. My heart, for one."

I could have just melted right then and there. "Even after seven years?"

"Especially after seven years." He nudged my chin. "You also hold the key to your own happiness. It's a choice. I know these past few months have been hard on you. I'm willing to do whatever it takes to bring a smile back to your face. But I also realize that I can never truly make you happy. Happiness comes from inside."

He was right—I had to start looking on the bright side, starting with the fact that I was still alive.

"I'm sorry I've been so miserable lately. I've never been one to easily adjust to change. And the fact that I wasn't adjusting as well as I'd like only made me more miserable."

"You're a perfectionist."

"Unfortunately."

"Not unfortunately. That's the way God made you. You just have to stop being so hard on yourself."

I rested in his arms again. I wasn't good at not being hard on myself. Maybe, with God's help, I could change that. Right now, I felt eternally grateful for Kent and for God's intervention in sending him home early tonight of all nights. As I fingered the necklace between my thumb and index finger, my mind replayed the events of the evening.

"I knew you'd never expect me to plan something during the Super Bowl."

"I can't believe you were going to give up the biggest game of the year for me." I felt like ice-cold water had been splashed in my face.

"Of course. There are more important things in life than football."

I pulled back so I could look him in the eye. "Kent, I want to stay here in Boring. I want to help you with the pharmacy."

His eyes brightened. "You do?"

"I do. I know it's taken me awhile to adjust, but I do like it here in Boring. As long as our marriage is okay, I'm okay. Really, I don't miss the fast-paced life in Chicago. It was too easy to keep myself so busy that I didn't even know who I was, nor did I have time to really spend with God. I'll take Boring over busyness. I think God brought us here for a reason."

Kent grinned. "I think you're right."

He pulled me into a kiss.

"I'm now proud to announce the results of our election." Karen Jones opened an envelope. "The new president of our Homeowners' Association is Laura Berry!"

It had been three months since Hillary was arrested. I stepped up to the podium as everyone cheered. I'm not quite sure how this had all happened. After Donna was released from jail, she'd decided a career in politics wasn't for her after all. She just wanted to be a mom. And with Hillary behind bars, someone had to fill the position. The whole neighborhood had come together and written my name on the ballot, electing me against my will. I didn't mind.

"Thank you, residents of Dullington Estates. I'm very grateful to be serving as your new president. I want to thank you all for your support, and I want to let you know that I'm here to serve and to make this neighborhood the best it can possibly be. In my opinion, Dullington Estates is a place where anyone is lucky to live. I want to continue that tradition."

I wouldn't have nearly the time that Hillary had to put into the position, especially now that I was going to work at the pharmacy. It was the perfect situation: Kent and I would get to spend time with each other, he would get the help he needed with the business, and I'd have something to keep me out of trouble.

Besides, I needed something to keep me out of trouble. Kent and I had just found out we were pregnant.

I think the townspeople were right—Boring was going to be the perfect place to raise my child, yawns and all. It's just too bad that I almost had to become a desperate housewife to see the town's value.

"Residents of Boring, you are what America is all about. You look out for one another, you care about your community, and you value the morals that have made this country great. You are the epitome of all that is good and decent, and I'm honored to serve you."

And you know what? I meant every word of it. Boring, Indiana, was the best thing that could have happened to me and to Kent. I was grateful to be a part of this community.

There was just one thing: I would never, ever eat pork rinds again.

Made in the USA
Lexington, KY
10 March 2013